"I want you."

The tiniest of shivers trembled through Madison.
"I know."

"Wrong time, wrong place?" he guessed.

"I don't do brief affairs."

"What if it turns into more than that?" He couldn't
help himself. He cupped her head and drew her
close enough for another kiss. "Are you willing to
explore the possibility?"

Day Leclaire and her family live in the midst of a
maritime forest on a small island off the coast of North
Carolina. Despite the yearly storms that batter them and
the frequent power outages, they find the beautiful climate,
superb fishing and unbeatable seascape more than adequate
compensation. One of their first acquisitions upon moving
to Hatteras Island was a cat named Fuzzy. He has recently
discovered that laps are wonderful places to curl up and
nap—and that Day's son really was kidding when he named
the hamster Cat Food.

Look out for an exciting, brand-new trilogy by
award-winning author Day Leclaire:

The Provocative Proposal (August 2001, #3663)
The Whirlwind Wedding (November 2001, #3675)
The Baby Bombshell (February 2002, #3686)

Coming Soon!

THE MARRIAGE PROJECT
Day Leclaire

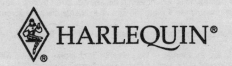

TORONTO • NEW YORK • LONDON
AMSTERDAM • PARIS • SYDNEY • HAMBURG
STOCKHOLM • ATHENS • TOKYO • MILAN • MADRID
PRAGUE • WARSAW • BUDAPEST • AUCKLAND

To those who make the tough choices.

ISBN 0-373-03651-5

THE MARRIAGE PROJECT

First North American Publication 2001.

Visit us at www.eHarlequin.com

Printed in U.S.A.

PROLOGUE

HARRY JONES sat in the middle of an office the size of a small house while controlled chaos exploded around him. Close to a dozen VPs and department heads crowded in front of his massive desk, each with a problem of absolute urgency and each needing an immediate answer to that problem. Flicking his pen across a document, Harry sent it spinning down the expanse of mahogany, reducing the number of people clamoring for his attention by one.

At his elbow his private line let out a demanding chirp and he tucked the receiver to his ear with an uplifted shoulder. "Talk to me," he ordered.

"Busy?" his father asked cheerfully.

Harry gave the door to his office a pointed stare and jerked his head in that direction. That's all it took. That's all it ever took. Every last one instantly obeyed his silent command, filing from his office with impressive haste.

"What's up, Dad?" he asked.

"I have something here that might interest you."

Harry leaned back in his chair. "I have to give you credit. You do come across the most fascinating bits and pieces of information."

"It's my job, remember?"

"Funny. I thought your job was promoting *The Principles of Love*. Speaking of which, how's the book tour coming along? Where are you? Seattle?"

"Portland. Seattle is tomorrow. And the tour is fantastic. Never had so much fun in my life. You were right

5

about all this handshaking and public speaking being up my alley. I guess I'm just a frustrated old salesman, or something.'' There was a notable pause and then Bartholomew said, "But that's not why I called."

"I figured as much. What's going on?"

"I received an intriguing document that I thought you'd find of interest."

"Can you fax a copy?"

"Only if I can send it over your private line. I don't want to risk anyone seeing the thing."

"Why?"

"It involves the Sunflowers."

"Dammit, Dad. You know I'd rather not get involved in your personal relationships—''

"This isn't about Sunny. It's about her granddaughter, Madison. I think once you read it, you'll decide to join me in Seattle."

"It's that urgent?"

"Yes, it's that urgent. Come on, son. Use some of that power I've seen you wield. Delegate the smaller jobs and get on this."

"I don't have any small jobs," Harry replied dryly.

"Right. How silly of me to forget. My son is Harry Jones, economic genius and corporate troubleshooter." There was no mistaking his teasing tone. "I bow down in tribute."

"Economic genius, corporate troubleshooter and terror of the financial world. And you cower at my feet, not bow down."

Bartholomew chuckled. "I stand corrected. Listen, take a look at what I send and decide for yourself. But I'm guessing you'll be on the next plane to Seattle."

Five minutes later the fax came through. Harry sat at his desk and read over the information and discovered his father was quite correct. He would be on the next plane to Seattle.

CHAPTER ONE

The Ten Principles of Love
by Bartholomew Jones

Principle 1: Sometimes it only takes one look...

MADISON ADAMS snapped open the ringing cellular phone with practiced ease. "Talk to me."

"Madison?"

"Hi, Aunt Dell. Lost again?"

"I hate to bother you, dear."

"It's never a bother," Madison reassured with absolute sincerity. "That's why I get paid the big money."

"It has nothing to do with the money and we both know it. You love looking after all of us, don't you, dear?"

Madison grinned. "I have to admit, it's more than a job. It's a calling. Now describe your location to me. I don't suppose you see any street signs nearby?"

"You'll be so proud of me. I'm standing at a street corner. Union and...and Fifth."

"This will be an easy one, Aunt Dell. Lift up your hand and flag a cab."

"Dearest?"

Madison sighed. "No money?"

"I was so careful to save enough to get home. But the most delectable latte called my name."

"I understand. Hang on, Aunt Dell. I have another

8

call coming in.'' She hit the flash button. ''Talk to me. Yes, Rosy, what is it?''

''Harley has an emergency.''

''Harley always has an emergency. What is it today?''

''Something to do with a Mercedes and a limited time offer.''

''Tell him that's not an emergency. Blood and maiming are emergencies. Cars come under the heading of our weekly meetings and they come in very low on the agenda. Make that clear, won't you?'' she instructed her assistant. ''Low priority.''

''He won't show at the meeting if I tell him that.''

''Then I guess we won't have to worry about any emergencies involving Mercedes, will we? Listen, I've just left Sunny's apartment and I'm on my way to the office, but I have a quick job for you to take care of before I get there. Call the local cab dispatcher for Aunt Dell.''

''Do they need to be on the lookout for her or just pick her up?''

''Pick up at Union and Fifth. Tell them to put the fare on my tab along with a generous tip.''

''Got it.''

Madison switched back to her aunt. ''Aunt Dell? Go ahead and flag down a cab.''

''Thank you, dear.''

''You're—''

To Madison's annoyance the phone went dead. It was the third occasion this month it had stopped working for no apparent reason. The family had been in an uproar on the last occasion when they hadn't been able to reach her. Fortunately, this time she was only minutes from her office and another phone. Stabbing at the call button for the elevator, she turned her attention to the book her grandmother, Sunny, had given her over lunch. She had five minutes to spare between Sunny's apartment and the office. That should provide ample opportunity to form an opinion. Not that she needed more than two of those five minutes.

"This is the worst piece of tripe I've ever read," Madison muttered beneath her breath. "How anyone can buy into this nonsense is beyond me."

A small ping announced the arrival of the elevator and without missing a beat, she turned another page and stepped into the car. "I can't begin to imagine what Sunny could be thinking. *Love can strike at the most inconvenient times. When it does, there's nothing you can do but surrender to its overpowering force,*" she read aloud. "Total twaddle. Bilge, drivel, malarkey, not to mention poppycock."

The car rose and Madison glanced up with a frown. The numbers above the door blinked rapidly as they ascended. This was *not* the direction she'd intended to go. Someone had made a mistake and she wasn't the least bit happy about it. Just as she opened her mouth to voice a complaint, the elevator shuddered to a halt and the lights winked off.

She groaned. "This is not my day."

"Nor mine," agreed a rich, masculine voice from the back of the car.

The sound startled her. She'd been so preoccupied with her book, she hadn't even realized there was anyone else on the elevator with her. "You'd think in a brand new office building they'd have elevators that work properly," she ventured.

"Conversely, the very fact that it's brand new may be why the mechanics are off. They haven't had an opportunity to fix all the bugs."

Madison's frown returned. "The elevator wasn't even going the right way."

He took a moment to digest that. "Elevators only go the wrong way when you don't pay attention to which direction the arrow is pointing."

It was a reasonable if unpalatable observation. She hadn't been paying attention. Nor was it the first time she'd taken unnecessary detours on an elevator—or in life, for that matter. She'd have to make a note to pay closer attention. No doubt it would join all the other notes, each with a similar message. It wasn't really that she didn't pay attention. The truth was she had phenomenal powers of concentration. Unfortunately, she tended to ignore anything that didn't directly relate to the task at hand. Whatever happened to be her current concern received her full focus.

Emergency lights came on with a wasplike buzz, coating everything in a jaundiced shade of amber. Madison turned to address her companion-in-disaster just as a loud pop echoed in the small confines. An ominous sizzle followed and the emergency lights faded.

"I hope you're not the screaming type," the man said.

"Certainly not," she retorted, firmly ignoring a warning prickle of nervousness. "I'm the most practical person in my entire family."

"Depending on the family, that might not be saying a whole hell of a lot."

Maybe if she listened very carefully to every word he spoke the nervousness would vanish. Now what had he said? Something about her family and a characteristic that would be laughable if she weren't so on edge. "You're right about that. It's not saying a lot. To be honest, my family consists of the most impractical individuals ever assembled in one group."

"Unfortunate." He paused a beat. "Please tell me you're not like them."

Focus! "Not in the least." It would take more than a dark, suffocating elevator to disconcert her. A lengthy stay might do the trick, but she could handle...oh, say...one or two minutes without losing it. Five, if pushed.

"Excellent. Now that we've established that you don't intend to scream or faint—"

"I never said a word about fainting," she corrected. "I just said I wasn't the type to scream."

A heavy sigh issued from deep within the car. "Are you prone to fainting?"

"No."

"Excellent. Now that we've established that you won't scream or faint, perhaps we can find a phone to call for help."

"That might be difficult since I can't see a blasted thing." How many minutes had passed? Two? Three? Her hands closed into fists. That gave her a whole one hundred and twenty seconds—if she were lucky one hundred and eighty—to get out of her predicament. Plenty of time to escape their prison before something unpleasant happened. "I don't suppose you have a cell phone on you? Mine stopped working in the middle of my last call."

She heard him shift in the darkness, a faint patting sound suggesting he was checking his pockets. "I must have left it in my hotel room. I'm not sure it would even work in here."

"The way our luck is running, probably not. How about a flashlight? Two-way radio?" Desperation was definitely kicking in. "Rappeling equipment?"

"Sorry. Left all that in my Superman cape."

The comment provided a much needed distraction. He sounded like her uncle, Daniel, who suffered from a severe Superman complex. Though he didn't carry it so far as wearing tights and a cape, he did get into trouble rescuing "damsels in distress," most of whom didn't want to be rescued. Fortunately, the lawyer she had on retainer gave a discount for volume usage. With her family, that proved a distinct advantage.

Madison swallowed hard and forced herself to follow the conversational gambit. "At least you have a Superman cape. I've found it's rare in this day and age."

"Let's just say I didn't have any choice in the matter. There's got to be a phone here, somewhere." She could hear him make his way across the car toward the control panel. "If I can... Got it."

She gave him a full two seconds to take care of the problem. Ample time, in her opinion. "Well? What are they saying?"

"Nothing, yet."

Silence reigned for an additional eight impossibly long seconds. If her knees hadn't locked up on her, she'd have crossed the car and snatched the phone from him and taken care of the situation herself. "When are they going to get us out of here?"

If her impatience annoyed him, he didn't let on. "No time soon. The phone's dead."

She didn't bother to disguise her alarm. "How can that be?"

"At a guess I'd say whatever's wrong with the elevator, the lights, and the emergency backup system, has also affected the phone."

"So we're trapped here?" The full impact of that question and its probable response settled over her like the smothering weight of a wool blanket. A wet wool blanket. She clutched the railing circling the wall of the elevator and held on for dear life. "There has to be a way out of this."

He turned in her direction, the sound of his voice pitched to soothe. "I thought you said you aren't the type to panic."

"I'm not panicking! How can you possibly think I'm panicking when I'm not? *Does this sound like panic to you?*"

"My mistake. I think it was the hint of hysteria in your voice that fooled me."

"Don't be ridiculous. I've never had hysterics in my life." She fought to draw breath. For some reason she found it difficult. "I think the air has stopped, too. It's getting warm in here. Don't you think it's warm in here?"

"What's your name?"

What did that have to do with how much air they had left? "Madison."

"I'm Harry."

Harry. A nice, safe, average Joe sort of name. She liked that. Right now she needed someone with those qualities. "I don't suppose your last name's Houdini?" As a joke, it was weak. Perhaps it was oxygen deprivation. The lack of air had stolen what little wit she still possessed.

"Actually the name's—"

"I need to get out of here," she interrupted. Didn't the man understand that? She'd been fortunate to get nice, safe and average, but unfortunate enough to get someone short on brain power. *"Now."*

"I'm afraid that's not going to happen. Tell you what, Madison. Why don't we both sit down and relax? We can talk while we wait to be rescued."

"Talk." Her brows drew together. "Doesn't that use up oxygen faster?"

"We're not going to run out of oxygen. I promise."

There was a hint of amusement in his voice that Madison found distinctly irritating. "And if you're wrong?"

"Then you can say I told you so. Assuming there's enough oxygen to say it."

He was definitely laughing at her. How annoying. Nothing about this day had gone right so far and it didn't look like it would improve anytime soon. She took a moment to stew over her options. She could continue to amuse him with her fears. Or she could release her current frustration by shrieking for help. Considering her lung power she might find that choice as amusing as he found her. Or she could sit down as he suggested and conduct a calm, rational conversation until someone showed up to rescue them. It didn't take much thought to choose the most reasonable of the three options.

Alarmed to discover she was shaking, she lowered herself to the carpeted elevator floor and leaned against the wall. Judging by the faint rustling emanating from the far side of the car, Harry had followed suit. She laced her hands together and fought to recover her equilibrium. She'd never lost control before. Not ever. It frightened her more than she cared to admit, perhaps because it had hit so unexpectedly. She took several deep breaths, relieved to discover it helped.

"What would you like to talk about?" she asked in a voice that approached normalcy. At least it no longer betrayed the crushing claustrophobia that had caught her by surprise. She didn't understand how she could experience such an irrational reaction. It didn't make the least bit of sense. But then she'd never been trapped in a darkened cage before.

"You were reading when you got on the elevator. I gather from what you were saying that you didn't care for the book?"

"No."

"Short and succinct, but not very illuminating. What's the title?"

He was struggling to keep their conversation going. The least she could do was cooperate. Focus, she reminded herself. "It's called *The Ten Principles of Love.*" How in the world could Sunny have bought into such nonsense? "And no, I don't care for it. It's total—"

"'Twaddle.' Not to mention 'bilge, drivel, malarkey,' and I believe you said…'poppycock.'"

"You overheard me," she accused.

"It was a little hard not to. You were speaking out loud." She heard the rustle of clothing and guessed he'd removed his suit jacket. Another silky whisper warned that his tie had followed. "If you think the book is so bad, why did you buy it?"

He had a delicious voice. Rich. Dark. Appealing. If their circumstances had been different, she wouldn't have minded listening to it for a while. "I didn't buy it. It was a gift. And I'm reading it because I'm curious to find out what all the talk is about. I'm also curious—or perhaps concerned would be more accurate—because my grandmother has bought into the premise. Did I explain how impractical my family is?"

"I seem to recall you mentioning it. How far have you gotten in the book?"

"I read the first three pages."

He chuckled, a deep rolling sound that provoked an actual tactile sensation. "I gather from the way you say that, that you were less than impressed. Are you sure reading three pages is sufficient to form an objective opinion about the entire book?''

"It didn't take much more than a single page."

''And what, in particular, is wrong with it?''

Madison tilted her head against the wall and felt the knot in the pit of her stomach slowly unclench. Talking was proving beneficial, thank goodness. Or maybe it was Harry. He seemed to have a reassuring way about him. ''Where should I begin? There's so much material to choose from.'' She considered some of the choicer tidbits. ''Okay. How about this one? *The first time you set eyes on your potential mate there should be an instant chemical reaction. No chemistry, no mating!* Tell me, Harry. How do you suppose that's determined? And what sort of chemical reaction does this Bartholomew Jones mean? When I see an interesting man am I supposed to check my pulse, blood pressure and temperature to see if there's some sort of biological or chemical response?''

''Too clinical?''

''Oh, it's not that.'' If that were the only criteria, Harry would qualify as provoking a chemical reaction. He might be an average sort of man, but he'd gone out of his way to calm her fears and distract her with conversation. He couldn't help it if she found his voice intensely appealing anymore than she could help it that her nervous system had gone out of whack. ''It's simply impractical.''

''I gather being practical is important to you?''

''Vital.'' Perhaps that was why she found her claustrophobia so unsettling. It stripped away all she held most dear and forced her to deal with emotions she was ill-equipped to handle.

"Does that mean that you find love an impractical emotion? Or are all emotions impractical?"

"Uncontrolled emotions are impractical," she corrected. As for love... "I believe in love. I just have trouble with romantic nonsense like love at first sight."

Harry remained silent for a long moment. Then he said, "Tell me how you think love should work."

As she considered how best to answer him, the strangeness of their situation struck her. How odd to be conducting such an intimate conversation with a perfect stranger. Perhaps the darkness encouraged the sharing of confidences. Or perhaps the manner in which Harry had tried to allay her fears had made the difference. Whatever the cause, she couldn't remember ever having such a frank discussion with a man before, nor enjoying a conversation so thoroughly. Even her claustrophobia had eased, subsiding to a faint apprehension.

"First of all," she began, "love shouldn't consist of a list of ten fundamental rules published in some silly book written so the author can make a fortune off TV appearances. It's disgraceful. His target audience consists of naive, gullible women, desperate for love, seduced by a good-looking pitchman making promises he can't possibly fulfill."

"That doesn't answer my question. If the book is wrong, how should love work?"

She wished she could see Harry's face. A steely thread underscored his voice and she didn't understand what had prompted it. Men named Harry shouldn't have so much as a hint of steel anywhere about them. They should be puppy dog friendly, woolly lamb innocuous and kind to terrified women. If he didn't shape up soon, she'd be forced to hammer that point home in no uncertain terms.

"Love should be something that's built over time," she explained. "There should be a solid basis between the individuals, founded on mutual trust, admiration and compatibility."

"It sounds like you've come up with your own principles."

He wasn't far wrong. "I may have given it some thought," she admitted.

Maybe more than a little thought. After all, hadn't she devised a blueprint for the perfect man, the sort of individual she could love with every fibre of her being? It was a theme quite dear to her heart, if one she kept secret from the rest of her family. And yet, she felt comfortable expanding on it with a total stranger. How peculiar.

"As I was saying," she tried again. "Love should be founded on mutual trust, admiration and compatibility. This compatibility should cover emotional affection, intellectual suitability and a general respect. And admiration, rather than love, is important because—"

"You've never been in love, have you?"

That stung. "I've never found the type of love that book describes, no. But then, I don't really believe it exists. I think Mr. Jones is describing lust or infatuation or, most likely, wishful thinking."

"If you've never known love at first sight, how can you arbitrarily deny its existence?"

"Personal observation."

"Combined with that practical nature, no doubt."

"Have you ever been in love?" she shot back. "Do you believe in the sort of instantaneous love Jones describes?"

"I confess that I'm almost as practical as you."

"Really?" For some reason that delighted her. So he really was a down-to-the-bones, rational sort of Harry,

despite the rough-and-rumbly voice. Just as she'd
thought. Perfect. "Then you believe the same as I do.
This spiritual, everlasting love is nothing more than a
myth perpetuated by dreamers, foolish romantics, and a
few unscrupulous con artists."

"Not at all."

"I'm glad we agree—" No, they didn't agree. Impossible man! How could someone who claimed to share
her practical nature argue with her, particularly when she
was right? It didn't make the least bit of sense. "Wait
a minute. How can you—"

"I'm reserving judgment," he interrupted. "Because
I haven't experienced it myself doesn't mean it doesn't
exist."

"Piffle."

"Excuse me?"

"It's a word my grandmother, Sunny, uses," Madison
confessed. "I like it. It has a nice, defiant ring to it. It
also sums up my reaction more precisely than any other
word I know."

"Piffle."

An unexpected laugh escaped at the way he sampled
the word. "Slides right off the tongue, doesn't it?"

"I'd say it's more like trying to spit out a mouthful
of feathers."

"I guess it's not a man's word."

"Not even close."

"Still…" Her defiance came through loud and clear.
"It expresses my feelings about our discussion."

"About love, you mean."

For such an intelligent man, Harry possessed more
than a few cockeyed notions. Perhaps she'd have time
to set him straight before they went their separate ways.
She shivered. Not that she wanted to spend any longer

on this elevator than necessary, but she was enjoying their conversation. If nothing else, it was keeping her mind off their situation. *He* was keeping her mind off their situation, sweet man. Sweet, annoying man.

"Normally I like people who are direct and to the point," Madison informed him.

"Just not so irritating?"

She managed to laugh. "Should I regard that as an added bonus?"

"Consider the entire package an occupational hazard. At least, the direct and to-the-point part is work-related. Being irritating comes naturally."

"Really?" He'd snagged her curiosity. She hadn't pegged him as the irritating sort. Wrong on a few issues, sure, but basically nice. "What do you do when you're not trapped in elevators or being naturally irritating?"

"Prepare yourself."

Madison settled herself more comfortably on the floor, folding her legs against her chest and wrapping her arms around them. "I'm prepared."

"I spend my days conducting statistical analyses of economic structures and models."

"Impressive. What does it mean?"

"I'm an economist. I guess you could say I'm part economist, part accountant with a pinch of analyst thrown in for good measure. I take complicated data and interpret it. Then I explain the facts as simply and exactly as possible."

He couldn't have had a more "Harry" sort of job, unless he'd been a banker. Poor man. Did he mind being so average? "And who do you analyze these facts for?"

"I'm an independent consultant."

"Got it. So you explain your economic models to whomever pays you."

"You want the specifics?"

"I'd love the specifics." Anything to keep her mind off the walls that periodically snuck up on her, threatening to steal away the hard-won vestiges of her control.

"I consult with major corporations about economic growth and market trends."

She took a moment to digest that. "You tell people how and where to spend their money."

"Yes."

"Are you good at it?"

"Yes."

"Very good, I'll bet," she guessed shrewdly. It was a tendency of meticulous individuals.

"So I've been told."

"I have a confession to make. You and I have similar jobs."

She'd caught him by surprise with that one. "We do?"

"Well..." Madison forced herself to be as accurate as possible. "My consulting is on a much smaller scale than yours. And I do a lot more than give economic advice. Although the advising part does seem to take up an inordinate amount of my time."

"And are you good at it?"

She didn't see any point in being modest. "Yes."

"Very good, I'll bet."

Madison grinned. "I'm a natural. Or, so I've been told. Of course, it helps that I'm practical. I don't allow emotion to affect my judgment."

"And who do you work for?"

"Oh, I'm an independent consultant, too. But instead of consulting for corporations, I deal strictly with Sunflowers."

"Excuse me?"

"Sunflowers. That's our family name on my mother's side. I'm an Adams. That's where I inherited my practical streak—from my dad's family. They're all bankers and accountants and lawyers. I don't have much contact with them." She hurried over that part, unwilling to go into painful detail. "The Sunflowers have always been my main concern."

"And what do Sunflowers do?"

"They're not as easy to pigeonhole as my father's relatives. They're…" She shrugged. "They're whatever they want to be. You could say a whim doesn't exist that hasn't attracted a Sunflower."

"I see."

"Don't misunderstand," she hastened to add. "They're wonderful. Loving. Generous. Fun. Amusing."

"But not practical."

"Not even a little." She smiled fondly, her affection echoed in her voice. "It's their worst failing."

"A failing you make up for?"

"I compensate, I suppose."

"Overcompensate?"

She took instant exception to the question. "Most certainly not."

"Piffle."

"I don't know how we got on the topic of my family, anyway."

A ridiculous primness warred with an uncharacteristic grumpy note and she frowned at her reaction. What did it matter what Harry thought, anyway? She held a job of vital importance for a family she flat-out adored. If she tended to go a little overboard in her zeal to prove herself of use to the Sunflowers, it wasn't anyone's concern but her own. The arrangement suited those involved and that's all that mattered. What right did Harry have to stick his nose in her family business, anyway? Not to mention that he'd gotten it all wrong, drawing ridiculous conclusions that held no basis in fact whatsoever.

"We could go back to the other subject we were discussing, if you'd prefer," he offered.

Had he sensed her thoughts? She wouldn't be surprised. He was a perceptive individual. Practical people often were. "I can't even remember what that was," she confessed.

"We were talking about love."

Shoot. "I think we've exhausted that topic, too, don't you?"

"Not even close."

His voice had dropped, the intonation far too low and husky. She shivered in reaction, a hint of unease giving her pause. For the first time it occurred to her that she was trapped in an elevator car with a man she didn't know, a man with whom she'd been discussing fairly intimate topics. *Not practical!* a portion of her brain screamed. Despite the conclusions she'd drawn about him, he could be anyone. He could be a thief or a murderer or someone unethical enough to take advantage of their situation. She didn't often make errors in judgment about people, but considering she wasn't operating at full efficiency, it was conceivable she'd made a mistake this time.

The claustrophobia she'd experienced earlier returned full force. The intense darkness unnerved her, exaggerating the sound of her breathing. It came far too fast, in quick, shallow, panicked gasps. She could hear his breathing, too. It escaped with slow, steady regularity, carrying a strong, masculine edge. Was that even possible? Did men have a different mode of respiration than women? It sure seemed like it. His were manly-man breaths, Me-Tarzan, You-Jane sort of exhalations. Was it deliberate? Or did it emanate from some unconscious, testosterone-driven source that men weren't even aware of?

Idiot! she scolded. This was Harry the Economist. Mr. Practical. Mr. Safe. A puppy dog friendly, woolly lamb innocuous sort of guy.

And yet... Somehow it seemed not only possible that he was somehow seducing her with his breathing, but probable. Maybe he didn't even realize it was happening. She buried her face in her arms. Dear heaven! He could be unwittingly saturating the air with each lusty exhale and there wasn't a darned thing she could do about it but drag the sweet, passion-laden molecules into her lungs with each helpless breath she drew.

"You're afraid again, aren't you?" he murmured.

"Yes," came her muffled response.

"How can I help?"

She lifted her head. "Just stay right where you are." The statement escaped without conscious volition. It was also a dead giveaway.

And they both knew it.

CHAPTER TWO

Principle 2: The voice of love
can win the most stubborn heart...

HARRY took far too long to respond. "I see."

What in the world did that mean? "What do you see?" Madison demanded nervously.

"That you're afraid of me. It's rather amusing when you stop and think about it."

"I don't find it the least amusing." At least he hadn't realized that her fear had somehow gotten wrapped around a confusing mixture of attraction. She relaxed slightly.

"I apologize. It's not the situation I find amusing. It's that you'd be afraid of me."

"Why? Isn't there anything intimidating about you?"

"I'm very intimidating." He paused a beat. "On a business level. In person, I'm pretty innocuous."

That's what she'd thought. Harry had a presence, no two ways about that. But until recently she didn't feel threatened by it. He'd been wonderful toward her, right from the start. The moment he'd sensed her claustrophobia, he'd done his best to alleviate it. The fact that he'd gone out of his way to try and make her feel better should have told her something. Her breathing eased, the give-and-take far less panic-stricken. Maybe that explained the strange attraction she felt. It certainly didn't have anything to do with Bartholomew Jones and his

26

peculiar notions of instantaneous bonding and love at first sight. Thank goodness for that much.

"Do you think we could talk about something else?" she suggested. Anything that might take her mind off her foolish behavior. Then just to prove how her claustrophobia had stolen every remaining vestige of self-control, she asked, "Do you really believe in love at first sight?"

"Yes."

"Even though it's so impractical?"

"I realize it's out of character," he said with suspicious humbleness. "But, sure. I think it's quite possible."

"Then you agree with Mr. Jones? You buy into all this stuff about love being chemical?"

"I suspect chemistry plays a part. Think about it. Why are we attracted to one person and not another? There has to be some sort of subconscious or instinctive or chemical reaction happening."

"Is it happening now?" she whispered.

She couldn't begin to guess where the question came from. It simply spilled free of its own volition. Before she could snatch back the words, or soften them with a reasonable—if patently false—explanation, the phone in the control panel rang. Divine intervention at its best. She heard Harry make his way to the phone and answer it. There was none of the blundering or awkward scrambling she'd have expected because of the intense darkness. His movements were slow and sure and precise.

"Yes, we're stuck. No, there are two of us. Right. Hang on and I'll ask."

"What? What are they saying?"

"It's going to be a little longer before they can release

us. Is there someone you want them to contact? Family who'll worry about you?''

"I was on my way to the office. Could they call Rosy and let her know where I am? I'm sure my family's in a flat-out panic by now.''

Harry relayed the information along with the assistant's number, refused their offer to contact anyone for him and hung up the phone. Then he settled in his corner of the elevator. Should he tell Madison that it would be several hours before they fixed the problem? Probably not the wisest move. The past half hour had been tough enough for her. No sense in spooking her with the un-adulterated truth.

"Where were we?'' Harry asked. As if he didn't know. The chemistry or instant attraction or instinctive male-female push-and-pull had been humming between them like a live current. *Is it happening now?* she'd whispered. Hell, yeah, it was happening, whatever "it" was. And it had been from the start, a fact she'd have admitted if she weren't so damned stubborn—or apprehensive.

"I can't remember what we were talking about,'' she lied without a hint of compunction.

If there'd been any light, he suspected he'd have seen a blush vivid enough to rival Seattle's most glorious sunset. He considered calling her on the lie. After all, he'd already let her off the hook once when she'd demanded he stay put on his side of the elevator. He'd been the perfect gentleman about the incident, too, politely acting as though he believed it was claustrophobia or fear that had prompted the remark, instead of a chemical reaction to end all chemical reactions. This would be the second time he'd let her off the hook. She might not know it, but she wouldn't be given a third chance, a fact he'd make clear at the first opportunity.

He'd learned long ago that life didn't serve its delicacies on a silver platter. A man went after what he wanted, grabbing hold with both hands. Right now he wanted Madison Adams. Let her deny the emotions sparking between them if it made her feel better. Denying the truth wouldn't make it go away. It simply made it easier to be caught defenseless, a fact he'd take delight in proving soon enough.

At his continued silence, Madison broke into hasty speech. "So... How did you end up getting stuck on my elevator? You must have been in the building for a reason. I was here to have lunch with my grandmother, Sunny. She has an apartment on the fifteenth floor and was supposed to introduce me to this Jones character—the one from the book?—but he never showed. Figures, right? The good news is... Maybe I don't have to worry about their relationship. It's one thing to talk on the phone or communicate over the Internet. But when it comes to face-to-face and in person, that's a whole different ball game. Don't you think? Maybe he changed his mind about flying out to meet her."

Harry waited until she ran out of breath before responding, choosing to answer the most innocuous of her questions and comments. "I came here for a meeting."

"Oh. Consulting with someone on economic structures and models?"

"I was asked to, yes. I haven't decided yet whether I'll take the job."

"Is it a big corporation?" A hint of excitement threaded her voice. "Perhaps a certain gentleman who deals in computer software? Or... Who else has corporate headquarters in Seattle? Could your meeting have to do with airplanes, maybe? How about a national coffeehouse chain?''

He smiled at her avid curiosity. ''I've been known to deal with companies that size, but not this time. I've been asked to examine a very small group as a favor for my father. I guess you could call it a working vacation.''

''Oh.'' She sounded disappointed. ''No doubt they'll be very grateful to have a man of your caliber look them over.''

''Would you be? Grateful, I mean?''

''The situation wouldn't arise. As I explained, I have everything in hand,'' she assured. ''But I'm certain this small group will benefit from your expertise. Not everyone can be as clever at predicting economic growth and market trends as the two of us. Once they realize how much better off they'll be, those in charge will be delighted to listen to what you have to say.''

He leaned his head against the wall and swore beneath his breath. ''What if the person managing this small group feels the way you do? What if he thinks he's doing fine without my input?''

''With your credentials you'll have no trouble convincing him.'' Her absolute confidence amazed him. ''He'll have no choice but to acquiesce to your superior knowledge and abilities.''

''I'd rather not throw my weight around.''

''Oh, right. You did mention that you were intimidating when it came to business.''

''Very intimidating,'' he reminded her.

''You weren't supposed to make me nervous, remember?''

''And now I am?'' Her complaint made him smile. ''Should we change the subject again?''

''No. I guess I can handle a small amount of ner-

vousness. Besides, I'd like you to explain something."
She shifted in the darkness, the faint scent of her perfume slipping across the car to wrap him in soft feminine
sweetness. "When you want to throw your weight
around, how do you go about it?"

Amusement vied with an intense flash of desire. "You
sure this discussion won't make your claustrophobia
worse?" he asked.

"Oh, no. Our discussion will help my claustrophobia." She hesitated, as though scrambling for an excuse.
"It'll take my mind off it."

She was interested in him as a man and doing her best
to hide the fact. Not that her best was all that impressive.
Apparently possessing a practical nature didn't include
subtlety or deception. He wished he could see if her face
was as easy to read as her voice. He was willing to bet
he'd find her expression as open and candid as everything else about her.

"If telling you about my work situation will prove
beneficial, I guess it's my duty to keep the conversation
going," he murmured.

"Yes, please. Come on, spill. How do you intimidate
people? I assume you don't always have to?"

"No." He opened the first few buttons of his shirt
and changed his position. Not that it helped. The floor
of an elevator wasn't the most comfortable place to
lounge for hours on end. Fortunately, the company more
than compensated for the lack of a chair or couch.
"Most businesses want my opinion and pay well for it.
But occasionally there's a job where the principal owners are squabbling or there's a high-level management
struggle going on. So they call me in to settle the financial end of matters and offer an opinion. In those cases
my presence is a source of conflict."

"Not very pleasant. How do you handle a situation like that?"

"First, I send an announcement."

She chuckled. "Something along the lines of, 'Prepare yourself. I'm coming'?"

"You got it. I send very specific instructions detailing what I'll require when I arrive. A nice long, nasty list. Hotel arrangements. Office space. Meeting times. Staff. Everything's terse and to the point."

"In other words, you rattle their cages."

"I prefer to think of it as getting their attention."

"And then?"

"And then I show up. Early. Most places that are in turmoil have been so busy arguing about how to accomplish my instructions that they're caught off guard."

"Let me guess. They spend the next couple of days bending over backward to make up for a bad first impression."

"By which time, I've been able to fully assess the situation and personnel and come up with a financial strategy. I can tell them what will happen if they don't make any changes and what will happen if they implement some of my changes and how they'd benefit best by doing precisely as I recommend."

"I assume most of them choose your final option?"

"Most. But not all." He shrugged. "And in a few cases, it's too late. Some things aren't fixable. It's as simple and unfortunate as that."

Silence reigned for several minutes while she absorbed his comment. "Speaking of the unfixable. How much longer do you think it'll be before they repair the elevators?"

"A while." He frowned. "Are you nervous again?"

Maybe he shouldn't have told her about his intimidation methods.

"Just a tiny bit." She rubbed her arms with swift, abrupt movements. "I thought it would get stuffy in here. But I'm cold. Isn't that crazy?"

"Would it make you feel better or worse if I sat with you?"

"I'm not sure."

"Would you like to try and see?"

Her hesitation roused his protective instincts, instincts that vied with the urge to go after what he wanted. Resisting that stronger, darker urge proved next to impossible, but he succeeded. Barely. He might chase his desires with every ounce of determination he possessed, but never at another person's expense. Especially not a woman caught between desire and fear.

She chose that moment to agree, unwittingly intensifying the silent, internal battle he waged. "Okay. Let's try sitting together."

"Let me get my coat. That should help warm you." He spoke as he moved so she could track his progress. Spooking her now wouldn't be his wisest course of action. "Say something so I don't accidently step on you."

"I'm here."

He crouched nearby. "And I'm right next to you."

"I can hear you breathing."

"Yeah, well, it's sort of automatic with me."

She laughed at that, the sound a bit edgier than he'd have liked. "I'm being an idiot."

"No, you're not." He sat beside her, leaving a gap of a couple of feet between them. No doubt she'd appreciate his restraint, if not the frustration that restraint exacted. "My mother was claustrophobic."

That caught Madison's attention. "She was?"

"Yup."

"How did she handle it?"

"Not well. I gather that elevators don't bother you under normal circumstances?"

"I've never liked them, but they've never sent me into hysterics before."

"You don't know how lucky you are." Though right at this minute, he doubted she considered herself any such thing. "Mom couldn't ride in one without me or Dad. I can remember as a little kid Dad would sort of scoop her into his arms and she'd close her eyes and hang on until we were out again."

"Poor woman. What did she do when your dad wasn't around?"

"She'd hold my hand and have me talk to her the whole way." That single act had instilled an overprotective instinct that troubled him to this day—especially when it interfered with achieving his objective.

"Talk? Like you are now?"

"Yes." He wished he could see her. He'd never realized how much he used body language and facial expression to analyze a person's thoughts and attitude. "Are you still cold?"

"I'll survive."

"Here." He shook out his suit jacket and handed it to her. "This should warm you."

She fumbled in the dark for several seconds and he reached for her, his hands colliding with hers. "Let me help." With a gusty sigh, her hands fell away and she held still. Ever so gently he draped the coat around her shoulders. To his surprise, she scooted closer and he wrapped his arm around her. Strike three, came the errant thought. Only, instead of being out, she was caught.

"You feel sort of big," she commented, clearly surprised.

"There's a reason for that."

He sensed her smile. "Is the reason that you *are* sort of big?"

"Not sort of, I'm afraid. Definitely big."

"I thought you said you didn't look intimidating."

"I didn't want to make you any more nervous than you already were."

"I see." She paused. "Thanks, Harry."

"Anytime."

"You know what?"

"What?"

"I've been thinking about this and I've concluded that being claustrophobic isn't the least practical."

He allowed himself the briefest touch, a quick reassuring stroke across her temple. Soft curls twined about his fingers in a welcoming caress. "I'm sure you'd control it, if you could."

"You may not have noticed, but my name's not practical, either."

Reluctantly, he untangled his fingers from her hair. "Maybe you take after the Sunflower side of your family a little more than you thought."

"Don't try and cheer me up."

Interesting. "Would you like to be more like them?"

"Some days. Being practical all the time can be tough."

"It's a heavy responsibility," he agreed.

She turned into him, inching closer. "Sometimes being practical can mean you aren't able to take people's feelings into consideration."

An odd note had entered her voice, the tone haunted

by the ghosts of sad memories. "I doubt you'd ever do that," he said in an attempt to comfort her.

"Sure I would. I'd do anything and everything necessary to protect my family, even if it meant occasionally hurting their feelings."

"And why is that?"

"Because they love me even though I'm like my father."

"Is that a bad thing?"

She didn't answer for a long time. And then she said, "It's a very bad thing."

Hell. "Madison—"

"It's okay, Harry. Don't mind me. I don't usually dump on total strangers. I think it's because we're trapped and it's dark and my emotions are all mixed up. And maybe it's also because my family is going out of their way to be frustrating these days."

"In what way?"

Somehow his fingers had become entangled in her hair again. This time he didn't let go. "Oh, my grandmother's fallen for this guy who thinks he's a love expert. They've been conducting an affair over the Internet and now they've decided to meet. My uncle Daniel is being sued by a woman for being too helpful. And I have a cousin who calls every day with one emergency after another. The latest one is that he needs a new Mercedes."

"That's an emergency?"

"It is for him."

"And you take care of all these problems?"

Her head dropped to his shoulder. The fit was sheer perfection. "It's my job. Fortunately, I have an assistant to help me. Sort of."

"Sort of?"

"She's a Sunflower."

"I gather her idea of assisting differs from yours?"

"Dramatically. For one thing, she doesn't have a clue what the word discretion means. If I want to keep something confidential, I can't tell Rosy."

"Rosy Sunflower?"

Madison chuckled. "Has a ring, doesn't it?"

"It sounds like you could use a little advice on how to handle your family."

She took instant exception to the comment. "Don't be ridiculous," she snapped, lifting her head. "There's nothing they can throw at me that I can't handle."

"Right." He reassured her with a quick, soothing touch. To his relief, she curled close once again, her head returning to its resting place just above his heart. "Silly of me to even suggest such a thing."

"That's okay. It's only because you don't know me very well." She gave his chest a reassuring pat. "Harry?"

"Still here."

"Thank you again."

He smiled at her formality. "You're welcome again. Madison?"

In response, she tilted her face upward a notch, her breath feathering his cheek in a strangely erotic caress. And then he committed the second craziest, most irrational act of his life—an inevitable one that came on the heels of dropping everything and flying out to Seattle over a simple intriguing document.

He kissed her.

She inhaled sharply, stealing the air from his lungs. Her spine went rigid and for a split second he thought he'd made a terrible mistake. He started to release her when she sighed, relaxing into his arms and giving him

back his breath in sweet surrender. Wrapping her up in
an embrace so possessive he didn't have a chance in hell
of disguising it, he drank in her taste, each kiss as ravenous as it was reassuring. Her hands splayed across his
chest, measuring the muscle-ridged breadth before curl-
ing into the crisp cotton of his shirt. She clung to him,
not giving any hint of hesitation or resistance.

If anything, she encouraged him, wriggling closer until they were cemented from shoulder to hip. Her lips
parted beneath his, soft and damp and slightly swollen
from his aggressive demand. He accepted the unspoken
invitation and delved inward, exploring with leisurely
intensity. The urge to imprint himself on her rode him
hard, but he resisted, unwilling to risk alienating her. The
emotions might run hot between them, but they were
also fragile.

They were in a unique situation. Being captured in a
cage of darkness had an odd effect on the senses. Life
swirled in a mad dash outside, while they escaped its
relentless influence. It gave them an opportunity to act
on impulses they might have otherwise ignored. That
didn't stop him from facing a few hard facts. If he started
something now, he'd be taking a huge risk, one he might
very well regret once reality put an end to this moment
out of time. Sure, he could push, forcing her to give way.
But how would she feel about it afterward? Would she
regret her actions? More likely she'd resent him for taking advantage.

He just needed time. He had a woman in his arms
who attracted him as no one ever had before. She was
soft and yet firm, confident while still painfully vulnerable, intelligent and yet frustratingly stubborn. And he
found every single quality more appealing than he'd
have thought possible. Once he convinced her they were

perfect for each other, life would be good. Life would be very good.

He cupped her face, sweeping her angled cheekbones with his thumbs. Her face fascinated him, possibly because he'd only caught the briefest glimpse of her from behind the book she'd been reading when she'd first stepped onto the elevator. Her chin was well defined, no doubt an outward reflection of her stubbornness, while her nose felt straight and elegant. She had wide-spaced eyes and long silky lashes. Her eyebrows arched strongly and her forehead was feathered with tight ringlets. He couldn't tell how long her hair was since she'd tied it up in some sort of intricate knot that rigorously subdued what he suspected would be a riot of curls. But she felt incredible in his arms. She felt like she belonged.

"Well?" she asked impatiently. "What's the verdict?"

"I'm satisfied."

"How can you say that when you haven't seen me?" she demanded.

"Are you trying to change my mind?"

"No. It's just—"

He caught her hand in his and lifted it to his face. "Your turn." Cautiously at first and then with growing boldness, her fingers slipped across each feature. He held still, strangely aroused by the sensation. "Well?"

She leaned into him, her hands forking through his hair. He caught the scent of her perfume once again, a light crisp scent that made him think of citrus and springtime. It took every ounce of self-possession to keep from tipping her off balance and into his arms. He balled his hands into fists, wondering if she sensed the rigid control he fought to maintain. Considering her complete focus was on other matters, probably not. He released his breath in a half groan.

"You have good hair, thick and springy," she finally announced. "What color is it?"

"That would be telling."

"Against the rules?"

"'Fraid so."

"Okay." She moved downward, exploring each fea ture once again. "Your brow has frown lines."

"Occupational hazard. I have to look intimidating, re member?"

"Right. I'll keep that in mind. Eyebrows…"

He decided to be helpful. "Two."

"At least it's not one," she retorted cheerfully. "Not quite Neanderthal, but they do have an aggressive qual ity to them."

"They match the rest of me."

"Oh, dear. As for the nose." Her touch was so soft it bordered on torturous. "Straight. No notable lumps or bumps. Either you weren't a fighter or you always won. Or more likely, no one could reach up far enough to sock you."

"I'm tall, but not that tall."

"Then which is it? Not a fighter or you always won?"

"I've always been a fighter," he warned.

She didn't take the hint. "Which means you won," she announced with smug satisfaction. "That doesn't surprise me. I'll bet you were able to talk your way out of most unfortunate situations. It's always best to use brain over brawn, especially when you're the bookish type. Now where was I? Oh, yes. Great cheekbones. Ouch. A hint of whisker."

"Sorry. I did shave."

"No need to apologize. I'm guessing your whiskers

are more aggressive than the rest of you. Next we have a firm no-nonsense chin and..." Her fingers spread across his mouth and stilled.

"And?" He nibbled at the tip of her index finger.

She whipped her hand clear. "And one mouth," she finished briskly.

"You can do better than that."

"One wide, hard—" her voice dropped to a husky whisper "—delicious, kissable mouth."

Resistance was no longer possible. He caught the lapels of the suit jacket he'd wrapped around her and tugged, propelling her into his embrace. She tumbled against him with a laugh. Sliding her arms around his waist, she found his mouth with unerring accuracy. His suit coat was in the way and he yanked it off her shoulders and tossed it aside.

She wore a silk dress, the distinctive material unmistakable beneath his palm. But it wasn't what he wanted to feel. He wanted her bare skin beneath his hands, to learn how she felt as thoroughly as he'd learned the contours of her face. To memorize each elegant dip and womanly curve. To test the weight of her breasts and the fullness of her backside. To uncover all the spots unique to her, the ones that would give her intense pleasure and leave her shuddering and eager in his arms.

"I want you."

His words impacted, provoking a slight hiccup in her breath, while the tiniest of shivers trembled through her. "I know."

Her tone carried far too much reluctance. "Wrong time, wrong place?" he guessed.

"Yes."

"And if it was the right time and place?"

"I'm not in the habit of making love to complete strangers on stuck elevators."

"You haven't answered my question."

"You don't live in Seattle, do you? This couldn't be anything more than a brief affair." She eased back. "I don't do brief affairs."

"What if it turns into more than that?" He couldn't help himself. He cupped her head and drew her close enough for another kiss. It was taking unfair advantage, but he didn't care. He wanted her and he'd use whatever means necessary to have her. "Are you willing to explore the possibility?"

"Yes, I'm willing."

Satisfied, he tucked her close. "Then we'll wait until the right time and place."

She released her breath in an irritated little sigh. "Kind of you to agree. Not that you had much choice."

"You'd be surprised at what choices I had."

Her head jerked upward, clipping his chin. "Do you really think you could have seduced me?" she demanded.

He rubbed his jaw. Served him right for being so arrogant. Not that it stopped him from further arrogance. "There isn't a doubt in my mind."

"I'm not that easy."

"Neither am I." He felt around until he found his coat and carefully returned it to her shoulders, tucking her close to his side once again. "I just know where that kiss was heading."

"It was only a kiss," she grumbled.

"Guess again."

"Come on, Harry. You're not being very practical about this. I'm not likely to be swept away by pure emo-

DAY LECLAIRE   43

tion and since we're so much alike, neither are you.
We're too smart to get caught in that trap.''

He grinned. "Keep telling yourself that, sweetheart.
Maybe you'll convince one of us.''

"Will they rescue us soon?''

Apparently she'd decided to change the subject. An
excellent option when you were losing the battle. Retreat
and find an easier war to wage. "Not much longer
now.'' He dropped a kiss in the middle of her curls.
"Try and relax. We'll be out of here before you know
it.''

"And then we'll go our separate ways.''

"We'll see.'' A companionable silence fell between
them, one he was reluctant to break. But there was a
final issue they needed to clarify and it was past time he
took care of it.

"Madison? You know... It's just occurred to me that
we never introduced ourselves.'' It wasn't quite a lie,
though close enough to make him uncomfortable. "I
think I should tell you my full name. It's Harry Jones.''

Silence.

"Jones," he emphasized. "Ring any bells? As in the
Jones from *The Ten Principles of Love*?''

More silence.

"Okay. Time for a bit of blunt honesty. I hope this
doesn't tick you off, but... Bartholomew is my father.''

Still more silence.

He cleared his throat, hoping to find a way to salvage
the situation. When he stopped and thought about it, it
was ludicrous. The man who'd faced down owners and
directors of multi-million-dollar corporations was intimidated by the prolonged silence of one highly practical,
overly protective, claustrophobic, half-a-Sunflower. "I
know I should have told you before this, but considering

how nervous you were, I didn't want to make it worse."
Why didn't she say anything? "Sweetheart?"

Her only response was a soft, delicate snore.

It took a few seconds for the truth to hit. When it did
he shook his head. Damn. This couldn't be good. The
minute she learned his name, she was going to be furi-
ous. And he couldn't blame her. He should have told
her sooner. He might have, too, except for one small
detail. He didn't want her to learn his identity until after
she'd formed an unbiased opinion of him.

Face it, Jones. The chances of Madison's opinion of
him being unbiased once she knew why he'd come was
remote to nonexistent. He grimaced. In fact, the only one
hundred percent certainty was that she'd never speak to
him again.

CHAPTER THREE

Principle 3: For the most perfect mating...
Take the time to explore all the senses
with your partner.

MADISON came slowly awake, wincing at the stab of bright light and the sudden explosion of sound. What the heck was going on? It took a moment for her brain to kick in, but once it did, she shot upright, escaping Harry's arms with telling haste. She stood poised in the middle of the elevator like a wild animal at bay, her eyes slow to adjust to the brilliant sunlight streaming in the car from the open door. A small crowd had gathered, staring with intense curiosity.

For some strange reason, she found herself turning toward Harry. But if she'd hoped for reassurance from that direction, her hopes were in vain. He still lounged on the floor, but instead of seeing the man who'd done his best to ease her fears, or even the man who'd kissed her with such passion, she discovered a creature who looked like nothing more than a huge, grumpy lion. Good heavens! Had she really chosen to sleep in his arms? If there had been any illumination at all, she'd have kept as far from him as possible.

He had a dangerously masculine appearance, the enticing features she'd examined with such innocent abandon having somehow rearranged themselves into tough-hewn planes and hard, uncompromising angles. There

45

was power implicit in every line of his body, the sort of power that came from brilliance of mind and strength of form and an indomitable will. All the time she'd thought herself caged with a sweet lamb of a guy, she'd really been caught in a snare with the king of beasts.

She folded her arms across her chest and glared in outrage. How could he have possibly described himself as innocuous? The thick hair she'd had nerve enough to thread through her fingers was a rich golden brown shot with streaks the exact same shade as a lion's pelt. Even his eyes reminded her of a caged beast, a shade of hazel enhanced with shards of jade.

"Well?" he demanded in an undertone. "Am I what you expected?"

Every feminine instinct she possessed urged her to flee the car. But since she'd always considered such instincts irrational, she foolishly held her ground. "You're nothing like I imagined. Worse, you went out of your way to hide the truth from me. That wasn't very nice of you. You're supposed to be a Harry."

"My name *is* Harry."

"Well, it shouldn't be. Harry's a safe name. And you're not the least safe. You should have been called something that warns people to beware. Like Hunter. Or Danger. Or Trouble. You also said you were an economist."

He sighed. "I am an economist."

"No, you're not. You're a lion. Shame on you. I don't appreciate your deception one little bit."

He slowly rose, shaking off all remaining vestiges of being a safe, normal man and filling the small space with his presence. Madison fell back a step despite her determination to hold her ground. How could she have missed him when she'd first stepped onto the elevator?

It didn't say much for her powers of observation. If it hadn't been for that darned book— She pulled his suit jacket more tightly around herself and the scent of him filled her nostrils. Instead of feeling more threatened, it served to reassure. This odor belonged to the man who'd protected her, not the intimidating stranger standing before her now.

"There's something else you're not going to appreciate," he replied. "I tried to tell you earlier, but you fell asleep."

"Another fact you neglected to mention?" As if pretending to be a lamb wasn't bad enough. "It's bad news, isn't it?"

"For you, yes."

"Harry! Madison!"

Harriet "Sunny" Sunflower pushed through the crowd and rushed to the door of the elevator, towing a large, handsome man behind. Not that he had much choice but to follow. Her hand was deep in the pocket of his suit jacket, which she held in a death grip, crumpling the expensive Italian silk. Based on the devoted smile tilting his mouth, he didn't appear to mind. His smile warned that he'd indulge Sunny's every whim. Considering how many whims Madison's grandmother enjoyed, that was saying a lot.

"I'm fine, Sunny," Madison assured. She edged around Harry and escaped the elevator.

"Of course you are, dear. After all, you had Harry with you."

It finally occurred to Madison that Sunny had used Harry's name, too. She turned and eyed her companion of the last several hours, an unpleasant suspicion beginning to dawn. "You know Harry, Grandmother?"

"Oh, dear," Sunny murmured. "You're upset."

"Grandmother—"

Sunny addressed the man she'd dragged along. "She only calls me Grandmother when she's upset. I can't begin to guess what I've done this time. I imagine I'm not supposed to recognize Harry. But since he's your son, I don't know why I shouldn't. Do you? Especially since we all met at the airport yesterday."

Sunny and her companion appeared to be of a comparable age, both in their early sixties and each exuding a warm, charming vitality that Madison knew from years of observation won devoted friends with careless ease. It didn't take much brain power to figure out who he was, Madison decided, which was just as well considering her brain cells weren't firing with their usual efficiency. No doubt this was the infamous Bartholomew Jones. Which would make Harry—

"I'm sure Madison will tell us what's wrong if you give her a chance," Bartholomew reassured Sunny.

"I assume you're Mr. Jones?" Madison interrupted. "I don't believe we've been formally introduced."

"My fault, I'm afraid." He offered his hand. "Please call me Bartholomew. And I see that you've already met my son. Sorry I missed out on lunch. The book signing ran longer than I'd anticipated. Harry did warn me we were going to be late. I sent him ahead to let you and Sunny know and offer my apologies."

Madison forced herself to take the time to shake hands before turning on Harry. He'd escaped the elevator, too, and stood looming behind her. Apparently something about his presence had discouraged the curious onlookers milling about in the lobby. The crowd had dispersed, offering them a certain amount of privacy. Not that she'd allow Harry's size to intimidate her the way it seemed to intimidate everyone else. Not a chance. She was on to his tricks.

"Why didn't you tell me who you were?" she demanded. "And don't try and say you didn't connect me with Sunny. I won't believe you."

"I knew who you were from the start. That's why I stayed on the elevator instead of getting off on your grandmother's floor. I thought you and I should speak privately."

"So you lied."

"I didn't go out of my way to identify myself, no," he admitted without apology. "You were nervous enough when we got stuck in the elevator without my making it worse."

"You deceived me. You let me ramble on and on about the book and my grandmother and all sorts of personal details without once warning me that I was making a total fool out of myself. How could you?"

"You weren't being foolish, merely a concerned and loving granddaughter." He folded his arms across his chest and stared down his straight, unbroken nose with an air of detached calm she could only envy. "I was also trying to keep you from having hysterics."

"I've never had hysterics in my life."

"You can thank me for that," he had the nerve to retort. "I kept you distracted discussing *The Principles of Love*. If I'd told you my full name, you wouldn't have been willing to speak to me and I'd have had the devil of a time getting your mind off our predicament."

"Isn't that wonderful?" Sunny interrupted. "They've been discussing the principles, Bartholomew. I see romance in their future."

Madison bit off a scream of frustration. "You do *not*

see romance in our future, Grandmother. Those stupid principles don't work. We're living proof of that.''

Sunny's face crumpled. "Oh, dear. Are you certain?''

Why did she always do that? Madison wondered in despair. At the first hint of adversity or criticism, her grandmother wilted like a flower. If Madison didn't know better, she'd have thought it was deliberate. "I'm sorry, Sunny. But the first principle is *Sometimes it only takes one look...*' Harry and I never even saw each other until a few minutes ago.'' She shot Harry an infuriated scowl. "And once I did, I realized a relationship would never work. He deceived me about his appearance. He pretended to be a lamb.''

"Funny,'' Harry muttered. "I seem to remember warning you that I was intimidating. Lambs are not intimidating.''

Sunny's anxious gaze shifted between them. "But you two did sit in there and talk, didn't you?''

"Well, yes—'' Madison confessed.

"And you were attracted to each other, weren't you?''

Madison hadn't seen the question coming and a fiery blush bloomed across her cheeks.

For some reason that cheered Sunny right up. "Silly girl. I told you the principles worked. You and Harry are proof positive, just as Bartholomew and I are. I have an idea. Why don't the four of us get together for dinner tonight? Seven, at House Milano. I'll give Joe Milano a call and arrange for a private table.''

"You can order lamb chops,'' Harry offered helpfully.

"Wait a minute,'' Madison protested. "How can you say the principles work? What are you talking—'' But Sunny and Bartholomew were already halfway across the lobby.

Harry unfolded from his stance by the elevator and snagged her arm. "She's talking about the second principle. If you'd read more than three pages of the book, you wouldn't have walked into that one."

"I'm almost afraid to ask. What's the second principle?"

"*'The voice of love can win the most stubborn heart.'* We may not have seen each other, but we did talk." He slanted her a grim look. "In fact, all that talking led to far more interesting pursuits. Thanks to that blush—not to mention a kiss-swollen mouth and a hint of whisker burn—they know it, too."

"I can't help blushing. It's not something I can control." She fingered her lips. "And if I have a swollen mouth and whisker burn, it's all your fault."

"I realize that. And you're welcome, by the way." He continued smoothly on before she had a chance to express her annoyance. "I also realize that if you could control any or all of those things, you would."

"Is that a crack?"

"Yes."

She considered pursuing that line of attack, then decided her energy was better spent on other, more immediate concerns. "I don't think we need to worry. They'll give up this nonsense once they see we're not interested in each other."

"And what makes you think we're not?"

She brushed that aside with a wave of her hand. "Don't be ridiculous. A few brief minutes of indiscretion on a stuck elevator does not make for a romantic relationship. I'd even go so far as to say a stolen kiss or two was obligatory. But it doesn't mean a thing."

"Funny. I seem to recall discussing an affair."

Another surge of uncontrollable warmth washed

across Madison's cheekbones. She really would have to find a way to curb that tendency. "Piffle. You were discussing," she retorted. "I was refusing. And now that I've had an opportunity to *see* the error of my ways, as it were, I'm absolutely, positively refusing."

"You can't refuse. We sealed our agreement with a kiss."

"Agreement?" She whipped around to confront him and discovered she had to look a long way up. Strange that the shoulders she'd found so comforting such a short time ago now appeared so intimidating. Not that she'd allow herself to be intimidated. Not a chance. That was for presidents and CEOs and owners of multi-trillion-dollar companies. But not her. "I most certainly did not agree to any such thing."

"You kissed me. Hell, sweetheart, you wrapped yourself around me and held on for dear life. If that wasn't reaching an agreement, I don't know what was."

More than anything she wanted to back down. Summoning every ounce of courage, she locked her knees in place and planted her hands on her hips. Sticking out her chin, she fixed him with her most ferocious gaze. The ridiculous image of a kitten spitting in the face of a lion took hold, one she had the devil of a time banishing. "I was suffering from claustrophobia. I wasn't in my right mind. You can't blame me for anything that happened in there."

"Oh, I don't blame you. In fact, anytime or anyplace you'd care to repeat what happened, I'd be only too happy to accommodate you."

"Really? How kind." If he caught her sarcasm, he didn't react to it. "Maybe the publishers should consider renaming your father's book. Instead of calling it *The*

Principles of Love, they should title it *The ABC's of Lust.*
Because that's all we experienced. Lust. Not love.''

"An excellent idea for a sequel. I'll mention it to
Dad.''

Did nothing faze the man? She decided to change tactics. "What are we going to do about dinner?''

"You mean what excuse should we use to get out of
it?''

Finally! She knew they possessed more similar characteristics than opposing ones. He must have reached the
same decision she had. "Exactly. You said you were
here on business. We'll use that as an excuse.''

"No, we won't.''

"Oh.'' She spared him a disgruntled glance. "Then I
can claim a previous engagement.''

"That's your choice, but I intend to be at that dinner.''

"You can't be serious.'' Didn't he understand the
problems that would cause? "They're already throwing
us together. This will only make matters worse. It'll encourage them.''

Harry shrugged off her complaint. "I want to have
dinner with my father. I happen to like the man. I also
like your grandmother and wouldn't mind getting to
know her better, too.'' He offered a smile that held far
too much appeal. Obviously he'd decided to pull another
intimidation tactic from his bag of tricks. "Come on,
Madison. What can it hurt? It sounds like a pleasant way
to spend the evening.''

She considered her options. If she refused to go now,
she'd end up looking petty. If she agreed, would it appear she'd caved under pressure? She'd have to risk it.
Better to keep an eye on Sunny and her love expert than
to allow their relationship to get out of hand.

"Fine. Sunny can't force us into a relationship in such

a short amount of time. It's not like we'll end up committed or engaged or anything.''

"Of course not. After all, we can't work our way through the entire ten principles over a single meal. Look at how long we were on the elevator. Hours, at least.'' His smile grew, taking on a predatory aspect that made her decidedly nervous. ''All that time alone together and we were only able to stumble through three of the principles. There isn't a chance in hell we can manage more than another one or two over dinner.''

That stopped her cold. She knew about the first two principles. How had they suddenly jumped to three? She cleared her throat. ''Just out of curiosity. What's the third principle?''

"For the most perfect mating, take the time to explore all the senses with your partner.'' His expression held a bit too much satisfaction. ''I'd say we've accomplished that one, too. Wouldn't you?''

Madison ran through a quick mental list. Sight. Hearing. Check and double check. They might not have seen each other until recently, but the final effect had been stunning. Then there was scent. An unbidden memory of his distinctive odor returned to haunt her and she suddenly realized she still wore his suit jacket. She whipped it off and shoved it into his hands, pretending she didn't notice his grin of satisfaction. Removing the coat didn't help. To her distress, she found she could still smell him. The very fact that his scent had somehow become a part of her, clinging both physically and mentally, warned of how unique she found him. Then there was touch. Oh, dear. They'd certainly done quite a bit of that. As for taste…

She spun abruptly on her heel. Kisses did not count as tasting. ''Kisses do not count as tasting.''

"They do in my book." Catching her by the arm, he turned her to face him and in front of everyone lingering in the lobby of the building, he tasted her again. "Congratulations, Madison," he murmured. "You've successfully completed the first three principles. And it's only taken three hours. I wonder if that's a record?"

"It can't be," she retorted in instant denial.

"Sure it can. How many more do you think we'll cross off by the time dinner's over?"

She pulled free of his arms. "None!"

"Guess again." His fingers stroked the curve of her cheek. "Fight if it makes you happier, sweetheart. But I'll have you in the end."

"I won't be intimidated by you, Harry."

He nodded in approval. "Good. I don't want a woman I can intimidate. I want a woman who's my match."

He didn't give her an opportunity to reply, which was just as well, since she hadn't a clue what she'd have said. Snatching a final kiss—a kiss she found impossible to resist—he left her standing in the middle of the lobby of her grandmother's apartment building and walked away. Madison glared at his retreating back. It was a very large, imposing back, as impressive and appealing as the rest of him. She turned away.

Impossible man. It didn't matter how delicious she found his kisses, nor how well they'd progressed through the first several principles. She wouldn't allow a bunch of stupid rules to dictate her love life. There were more important considerations, considerations she'd delineated quite carefully in her personal journal. And not one of the characteristics on her list included how he should smell or taste or feel.

Not one.

She couldn't resist stealing a final glance at Harry.

Now that she reflected on the matter, maybe it wouldn't hurt to consider a few revisions to her blueprint. After all, experimentation led to improvement. And compared to Harry, her blueprint left something to be desired.

"Quiet, everyone," Sunny announced. "We have a lot to discuss and not much time."

"I can't be away from the office too long." Rosy spoke up. "Madison gets downright cranky when I'm not there to help."

Sunny gave a brisk nod of approval. "You make an excellent assistant. If it weren't for you, we wouldn't have known what to get Madison for her birthday. We're all very grateful."

A chorus of agreements came from the other Sunflowers and Rosy grinned. "Just remember that when it comes time for the big surprise I get full credit."

"Done." Sunny clutched Bartholomew's book close. "Phase one and two have been successfully completed. Harry came and the two have met."

"More than met," David said with a chuckle. "I don't suppose you arranged that elevator malfunction?"

Sunny smiled modestly. "The building engineer owed me a favor. Getting them both alone on the same elevator was the tricky part. But it ended up being one of my better efforts, I must confess."

"So what's phase three?" Dell asked. "How can we help?"

"It shouldn't be too difficult. Not for a Sunflower. Fortunately, Madison tends to be a bit oblivious to everything other than her current project."

"It's a regrettable trait she inherited from her father," Daniel offered.

Sunny dismissed the comment with an impatient
shrug. "Nothing we can do about that. Instead of be-
moaning the unfortunate influence, we'll use it to our
advantage."

"How?" Rosy demanded bluntly.

"We'll give her something important to focus on. And
while she's distracted by that, we'll put our plan in motion." Sunny beamed. "And I have just the perfect distraction. We're meeting at dinner tonight and I'll lay the
groundwork then."

"She'll be so pleased with our ingenuity."

"She'll thank us."

"This will be the best birthday yet."

Sunny quieted her relatives with an upheld hand. "After all Madison's done for us, she deserves the best present we can find. Having met Harry, I can happily confirm
that he's the absolute best. I think we can all be confident
that our little marriage project will meet with complete
success. We can also be confident that Madison will be
eternally grateful for our interference."

"Grateful enough to increase our allowances?"
Harley wanted to know.

Sunny grinned. "Trust me. I've taken care of that,
too."

Harry stood in the lobby of King Tower and watched as
Madison entered the building. He shook his head in disbelief. She had to be one of the loveliest women he'd
ever seen. Not that she seemed aware of that fact. Perhaps it had to do with her level of focus. Since her appearance wasn't important to her, she didn't give it more
than cursory attention. And yet, she exuded a careless
elegance that held intense appeal.

She wore her hair loose and he discovered that it was

longer than he'd thought. The dusky ringlets spilled over her shoulders and down her back in carefree abandon, framing her face and setting off the bright gold of her dress. She didn't wear a lot of makeup. Of course, she didn't need to. Her lashes were thick and black, drawing attention to large, inky-dark eyes and a generous mouth he'd explored for far too short a time. He'd have to correct that oversight. Soon.

He knew the instant she noticed him. There was a slight break in her stride as she approached and her eyes turned as luminous as starlight. Then her lashes flickered downward to curtain her pleasure. But there was no disguising the softening of her mouth or the way her breathing kicked up a beat. Even when she glanced up again, her wary regard betrayed an intense awareness of him as a man. She stopped several feet away, as though hoping the discreet distance would establish a ring of protection.

He demolished the ring with a single stride, invading her space and allowing all the chemical reactions she denied so fiercely to be set in motion. Masculine collided with feminine, sparking the air between them.

Harry took his time before speaking. "You came."

"Don't try your intimidation tricks on me," she ordered briskly.

He lifted an eyebrow in question. "Intimidation tricks?"

"You told me about them on the elevator, remember? Showing up early. Letting your size make people nervous. Staying quiet so everyone else rushes into speech and—" She broke off abruptly.

"And betrays themselves?"

"You are a difficult man, Harry Jones."

"Yes." He sympathized. "I am. We're a lot alike in that regard, aren't we?"

That cheered her right up. She immediately relaxed and slipped her hand into the crook of his arm. "Yes, we are. We're both difficult and both intimidating."

"Not to mention practical and logical."

"That's why we're so good at our jobs." She glanced around. "I thought we agreed to meet at House Milano. Isn't that at the top of King Tower? What are you doing down here?"

"I thought I'd ride up with you."

It only took her a moment's reflection to see through his explanation. "You weren't by any chance worried about me, Mr. Jones?" He couldn't tell if the idea pleased or offended her. "Were you concerned that I might have another fit of claustrophobia?"

"Not a chance," he lied with calm assurance, pushing the call button for the elevator. "This afternoon's incident was a fluke, an unfortunate combination of factors unlikely ever to happen again."

"But if they do, you want to be there?"

He chuckled. "Of course."

The elevator arrived just then and he followed her into the car. He couldn't help but notice that her breathing altered and the color ebbed from her cheeks. He'd have liked to snatch her close and kiss her from the first floor straight through until they'd reached the top. His mouth twisted. But that wouldn't be practical, or so he suspected she'd claim. Without a word he closed his hand around hers and began to talk—light, inconsequential conversation that didn't require too much thought or response. The minute they arrived at the restaurant, he released his hold. She flashed him a sweet smile of gratitude before stepping from the car and traversing the pathway of diamond-shaped, pink-and-ivory marble leading toward an imposing glass reservation desk.

"I meant to ask earlier." She was swift to regain her self-possession. "Have Sunny and Bartholomew arrived yet?"

"Not yet."

Madison nodded as though she'd expected as much. "They're giving us time alone in the hopes that something more might develop between us. I don't suppose that's another of your father's love principles?"

"As a matter of fact—"

"Mr. Jones, Ms. Adams?" An elderly gentleman dressed in a black tux with a white rose pinned to his lapel approached from behind the reservations desk. "Welcome to House Milano. My name is Georgio." He gave a courtly bow. "Mr. Milano has requested that you be given our very best table. If you'll follow me, please?"

They passed through the main dining area where the restaurant blended Old World charm with a contemporary flair. Walls of glass offered an incomparable view of downtown Seattle and tables had been set at discreet distances from each other, angled toward the dance floor where a combo played a delightful jazz number. Harry was impressed.

"I understand this is your first visit to our establishment." Georgio smiled in a friendly manner, a far cry from the more typical patronizing maître d'. "You'll find it's the perfect place to spend a leisurely evening."

One end of the room was divided off from the main area and Georgio led the way through a gated archway. Low dividing walls and barrels of plants separated the scattered tables, offering the diners both privacy and a stunning view of the city and Puget Sound. There was no question in Harry's mind that this section of the restaurant had been created with romance in mind.

"We reserve these tables for our special guests," Georgio explained in an undertone. "Sunny is one of Mr. Milano's favorites. A most delightful woman."

"Most people think so," Madison agreed.

"No doubt." He held out her chair. "Please feel free to visit our dance floor if you wish. I'll return shortly for your drink order. Mr. Milano has requested that I take care of all your needs personally."

Madison waited until Georgio left before speaking. "Harry?"

He didn't look up from the wine menu. "Try not to worry, Madison. It will all work out."

"What's going on?"

"My father and Sunny are being a bit overzealous. That's all."

"Overzealous?" Her eyes narrowed. "I know a setup when I see one and this is definitely a setup. Now what are we going to do about it?"

Harry closed the menu with slow deliberation and returned it to the immaculate white linen tablecloth before fixing Madison with a curious gaze. "What do you suggest we do?"

"We need to come up with a plan to stop them."

He lifted an eyebrow. "A plan to stop what, precisely? Tonight's dinner?"

"No. I think we both agreed that Sunny can't—"

"Or are you suggesting that the elevator malfunction was some sort of insidious plot to throw us together?"

"Don't be ridiculous." Her dress gleamed in the subdued lighting, the warm gold at odds with the irritation in her voice. "Of course I don't think that. Sunny's good, but not that good."

"I see. Then it's what we did on the elevator that has you all worked up."

"I'm not happy about it, if that's what you're asking." She didn't back away from a potentially uncomfortable discussion, he'd give her that. "Doesn't what happened bother you?"

"To be honest, it's what happened when we got off the elevator that bothers me more."

Her brows drew together. "What do you mean?"

"The woman I kissed vanished the second the lights came on." He leaned across the table, fixing her with a determined gaze. "And I want her back."

CHAPTER FOUR

*Principle 4: Fear can ruin even the
most promising relationship.
You have to decide what's more important to you—
Love...or protecting yourself from
life's bumps and bruises.*

MADISON didn't look away, despite the alarm that registered in the inky depths of her eyes. "I wasn't myself in that elevator," she claimed.

Harry wouldn't let her get away with that one. "Sure you were. You were more yourself this afternoon than at any other time. The darkness allowed you to be free of normal, everyday constraints. You just don't want to admit it." He tilted his head to one side. "Why is that?"

Pure passion broke through. "Do you blame me? Do you think I'm comfortable admitting that at the least provocation I'd kiss a total stranger in an elevator? That I'd curl up on the floor with him and...and—"

"And be tempted to have a brief sexual encounter."

He'd pushed too hard. Her spine tautened into a rigid line and she swiveled to inspect a view he doubted she actually saw. "It never would have gone that far."

"It could have. It still might."

"Not a chance."

He appeared interested. "Is that a challenge?"

"No!"

"It sounds like one."

"Would you please be serious?"

"I'm dead serious. You wanted me in that elevator as much as I wanted you. We both still feel the same way." He reached across the table and caught her chin in his palm, gently turning her to face him. "If we'd made love, we wouldn't be sitting here discussing it."

A hint of desperation vied with the need that burned in her gaze like black fire. "We wouldn't be together at all."

"Sure we would. We'd be in your bed or in mine, making love in a more comfortable setting. Because I guarantee, once would not have been enough for either of us."

"You're wrong."

"Am I?" He couldn't help himself. His thumb smoothed a path along her jaw. She'd felt incredible when he'd explored her features before. But now, watching as he touched her, seeing the desire soften her lips and bring a flush to her cheeks, witnessing it wash into her eyes and excite her body, hit him hard. If they hadn't been in a public setting he'd have done his level best to drive that passion to uncontrollable heights. "You're allowed to want me, Madison."

"No. It's not—"

His mouth twisted. "Practical?"

"Yes. No." She closed her eyes in frustration. "I can't do this, Harry. I can't afford to be distracted. I have a family to take care of. They depend on me."

"Your family isn't going anywhere. Nor are their problems. Do you really think they expect you to spend every waking day taking care of them? Even at the expense of having a life of your own?"

"That's not the point."

"You're right. It's not." He closed the distance between them and took her mouth in a lingering kiss. "This is the point."

"Harry."

His name escaped in a helpless whisper. This time when he leaned toward her, she met him halfway. Their mouths collided, mated and parted, then mated once more. They were back in the elevator, lost in a moment out of time. She opened to him, welcoming him with everything that was uniquely feminine—a soft sigh of intense pleasure, the eager parting of her lips beneath his, the blossoming of her special scent, the sweep of desire warming the skin beneath his hand. Only her guarded expression warned that her surrender wasn't a complete one. It was that ultimate reluctance that forced him to release her.

"Madison, why are you resisting the idea of having a relationship with me?"

She took a deep, steadying breath that suggested she was more affected by their kiss than she cared to admit. "There are a lot of reasons."

"Name them."

She didn't bother to hide her annoyance. "You're in your financial advisor mode again," she accused. "I'm not some sort of problem you can negotiate away."

"Good. I don't negotiate." He waited until his statement struck home before continuing. "Come on, sweetheart. Tell me the reasons a relationship between us wouldn't work."

"All right, fine." She ticked off on her fingers. "First, there's your father and my grandmother."

"How is that a problem?"

"They're dating. What if it doesn't work out? It complicates matters between us."

He dismissed that with a shake of his head. "I handle

complicated situations all the time. So do you. Besides, Dad and Sunny are adults. And in case it hasn't occurred to you, what they choose to do is none of our business.''

Her mouth compressed. ''Anything that affects a Sunflower *is* my business.''

''If I accept that Sunny is in agreement with that statement—and that's a big if—then there are two possibilities. Either my father and your grandmother will fall in love and marry, in which case they'll be delighted should we follow their example. Or they'll eventually part as friends. In which case what happens between us has no bearing on them.''

''How do you know they'll part friends?'' she protested. ''That's not how all relationships end.''

''They do in my family. What else?''

She looked like she wanted to debate his last point some more. No doubt she would have if she felt she had the necessary ammunition. But since she couldn't refute his claim, she wisely chose to move on. ''There's your father's book.''

''What about it?''

''I don't agree with it. I think it's—''

He cut her off without compunction. ''I believe we've already established what you think.''

''See? I've made you angry.''

''I'll get over it. In answer to your latest concern, I have every confidence that you'll eventually discover the error of your ways.'' He offered a wry smile. ''After all, we share a similar nature, as you've taken pains to point out. And since I'm convinced the book is right, you will, too, given time. What else?''

''I wasn't finished with my last objection,'' she argued. ''I have quite a bit to say on the subject.''

"No doubt. But I've decided we *are* finished discussing the book. Move on."

She snatched up the wine menu and buried her anger in its pages. She wasn't used to people defying her, he realized. And she didn't like it. Clearly, the Sunflowers had been too easy-going with her, allowing her autocratic nature free rein. She'd lost the ability to negotiate. He'd have to persuade her to see the advantages of a friendly compromise. Having one person always in charge, always the winner, wasn't the sort of affair he had in mind. It didn't make for a healthy work environment. Nor did it make for a healthy relationship in the bedroom—at least, not in his bedroom.

She poked her nose around the edge of the menu. "We're both too busy with work for a personal involvement."

He took the menu away from her. "If I can find time, you can. I'm sure Sunny will be happy to arrange with the other Sunflowers for you to have a few days free."

"Not a chance. My job is to take care of them and I refuse to shirk my responsibilities."

Enough was enough. They'd danced around the issue long enough. "So far all you've given me are excuses. There's something else going on, Madison. Some hidden factor I'm missing that affects this equation. You like being in control and you've made practicality the standard by which you measure everything. Why is that? I'm guessing that you've chosen this particular path for one of two reasons—either something happened to you, personally, or something happened to your family." Her reaction warned that he'd struck a nerve. "Which is it?"

The change in Madison was startling. All emotion vanished from her expression. Her eyes lost their dark luster, turning flat and remote. And an unnatural calm settled over her. Even her wayward curls stilled, as though leeched of their life's energy. "I have no idea what you're talking about," she blatantly lied.

He leaned toward her, pinning her with his gaze. "What the *hell* is going—"

"Are we interrupting something?" Sunny chose that moment to sweep down on them. She dropped a quick kiss on her granddaughter's cheek and another on Harry's. "Sorry we're late. But once we explain, I'm sure you'll understand."

"You're not interrupting a thing," Madison hastened to reassure her.

"Sure they were," Harry corrected, giving her a final, warning glance. They'd put their discussion on hold for now. But they would finish it—and soon. "I suspect we'll forgive them once we hear their news. What's up, Dad?"

Bartholomew grinned. "Congratulate us, Harry. Sunny's agreed to be my wife."

"Attention, everyone." Sunny called her family to order. The din from a dozen chattering Sunflowers faded. She peered through her reading glasses at the paper she held and nodded briskly. "All right, my dears. Here's the latest update on the marriage project. You'll be pleased to know that our plan has been set in motion."

"How did she react to your engagement?" Aunt Dell asked. "Was she as pleased as the rest of us?"

"I think pleased might be a wee bit of an overstatement. But don't let that worry you. She'll come around in due time." Sunny paced in front of her relatives. "Now I've been giving this a lot of thought and I've come up with the perfect way to implement our plan."

"I'm happy to help any way I can," Daniel stated,

"so long as it doesn't involve anything illegal. Madison says our lawyer isn't very happy with me, so I'd better keep a low profile. No helping. She was very specific about that."

"Not to worry, Daniel. I'm fairly certain we can do this without breaking too many laws. At least... They'll only be teeny tiny laws."

"What do you need us to do?" Harley frowned. "It's not going to cost a lot of money, is it?"

"No, my boy. My plan will only take time and a bit of creative thinking." She waved a paper in the air. "This is a sign-up sheet, everyone. Each of you has to pick a rule from *The Principles of Love,* one you think suits you best. Your job will be to demonstrate it for Harry and Madison—involving them in the course of the demonstration, of course. I'll go first so you get the idea."

"Which rule are you choosing?" Rosy wanted to know.

"I'm fairly certain Harry's already taken care of the first three all on his own. So I'll be generous." Sunny made a slashing notation on the sheet. "Not only will I reinforce those, I'll throw in the fourth rule, no extra charge."

"We have a serious problem on our hands," Madison announced.

Harry released his breath in a long, exasperated sigh. "And good morning to you, too."

"Oh, right." There were times when fixating on a particular problem or goal could generate a certain social awkwardness. This was one of them. "Good morning, Harry."

He swung the door to his hotel room wider. "Won't you come in?"

"Thank you." She crossed the threshold and turned to confront him. The sight of his business suit brought a frown to her face. "Oh, no. This will never do."

"What's wrong now?"

"Are you working today?" She hadn't anticipated that and should have. "Do you have an appointment with this group you told me about?"

"I was going to make a preliminary call, yes. But it can wait if you have something more important in mind."

That cheered her up. "Excellent. The first thing we'll need to do is get you out of this." She circled behind him and stripped off his suit jacket, tossing it over her shoulder. "The tie will have to go, too."

He folded his arms across his chest. "First explain what's going on."

"You're wasting time. And that's one thing we don't have." She continued around him and reached for his tie, working the knot. "You and I are going on a picnic."

"A picnic." He lifted an eyebrow. "A picnic where time is of the essence?"

The tie came free and next she applied herself to the buttons at his throat. "Blame it on Sunny. She didn't give me much warning." Madison paused, clutching the collar of his shirt as she considered. "You know... If it were anyone else, I'd suspect it was deliberate. This little outing came up with suspicious speed."

"Are you saying Sunny is devious?"

She glared in outrage. "Not in the least."

"Then we can safely assume this picnic is spur of the moment."

Madison fought off any lingering doubts. "Of course." She slanted Harry a quick, assessing glance as she applied herself to more buttons. "Your father won't mind Sunny's impulsiveness, will he?"

"Sorry to crush your hopes, but he won't mind in the least." He caught her hands before they could progress any further, pressing them firmly against his chest. "Are you finished undressing me?"

His heartbeat thundered beneath her palms and she suddenly realized how her actions might have been interpreted—or misinterpreted. His shirt gaped, revealing crisp brown hair and a hint of a chest she'd already discovered was impressively broad and muscle-ridged.

She snatched her hands away and stepped hastily backward. "Yes, I'm finished. All finished. Completely finished. As finished as it's possible to be. I'll let you take over from here." She motioned urgently. "What are you waiting for? Go. Get changed."

He didn't budge. "In a minute. First, you have a choice to make, sweetheart."

"Choice?" The word caught in her throat and she tried again. "What choice?"

"We can go on a picnic or we can continue what you've started. Which will it be? Indoor fun and games, or outdoor?"

She moistened her lips, horrified to discover that she actually had to take a moment to weigh her options. "Outdoor," she finally whispered.

"You sure?"

"Yes."

"In that case, wait here."

It wasn't what either of them wanted, but she summoned up the wherewithal to keep her strappy little sandals glued to the parquet foyer of his hotel suite. It dawned on her then that it *was* a suite, and quite a fancy one at that. Situated at one end was a kitchenette connected to a small, formal dining area. To her left she could see a room used as either a den or office and a huge living area with a spectacular view of Seattle and Puget Sound. It reminded her of their evening at House Milano. Harry had disappeared through a doorway on the far side of the living room, no doubt leading to the bedroom.

She itched to explore and when he didn't make an immediate reappearance, she gave in to her curiosity. The kitchen was fully equipped and she had the disconcerting impression the kitchen had been stocked with Harry's preferences in mind. She'd suspected from the start that he was good at his job, but perhaps he was even more important than she'd realized. A breakfast nook had just enough room for a small table. Place mats, dinnerware and cutlery for two had been laid in preparation for his next meal. She stared at the intimate setting for a long time. Did Harry have a traveling companion she didn't know about? Or had the table been set for two in case he chose to entertain a casual visitor. The thought was an unsettling one.

Escaping the kitchen, she crossed to the dining room. A hutch contained an elegant set of Lenox china and stunning hand-cut Bohemian lead crystal to be used for more formal dining occasions. Arrangements of fresh cut flowers overflowed the dining room table, as well as dotting various surfaces in the living room. The colors reminded her of Harry, strong greens and golds, accented with bold red peonies.

Glancing toward the office, she resisted the urge to explore any further. The desk revealed a laptop computer and an assortment of neatly stacked files and papers. She doubted Harry would appreciate her invading his work environment. Some places were sacrosanct and she respected that. Crossing to the bank of windows she examined the bustle of tugs and ships in the harbor, a bustle mirrored by the traffic clogging the Seattle streets far below.

"Would you like a cup of coffee?" Harry asked, appearing in the doorway that led to his bedroom. "I can't promise to fix it with the same skill as the local cafés around here, but I can promise it'll be drinkable."

Madison swivelled to face him and couldn't summon so much as a single word in reply. So far all she'd seen him in were suits, which had been intimidating enough. Now in a pair of low-slung jeans and a casual cotton shirt he'd become more dangerous than she'd thought possible. Perhaps it was because the suits had cloaked him in the domesticated garb of the business world, a world she moved in with complete comfort. But thanks to her, he'd shedded the trappings that made her feel at home and revealed his true nature. He was a lion, a fact she'd allowed herself to forget. Well, now the beast had been set loose and was on the prowl and she had no one to blame but herself.

"Madison?" He watched her with predatory intentness. "I assume by your expression, that's a yes to the coffee? Maybe even a 'hell yes'? And heavy on the caffeine, I'm guessing."

This had to stop! She couldn't afford to reveal a sexual interest in Harry. And that's all it was—sexual. "We don't have time, I'm afraid." She employed her best business tone of voice. Brisk. Efficient. Not a hint of the frantic need clawing at her. "We have a lot to accomplish in a few short hours."

"This is Seattle." He didn't give her a chance to argue, but simply anchored her to his side with a sweep of his arm and towed her from the room. "You of all people should know there's always time for coffee."

Once in the kitchen, he held her chair with unconscious ease, as though he'd performed the act on a regular basis. She took a seat, voicing a concern that had been troubling her since she'd arrived. "I thought you were here to advise a small group on financial matters."

He didn't look up as he prepared the coffee. Was it her imagination or did he hesitate before answering? "I am."

"You said they weren't powerful movers and shakers."

"No, they're not."

She hadn't been mistaken. He didn't want to discuss this subject for some reason. "How can they afford to put you up in such an expensive suite if they're such a fiscally small group?"

"They aren't responsible for my expenditures. As for the suite, the hotel upgraded my accommodations."

That sidetracked her. "Why would they do that?"

He shrugged. "I've done work for them in the past."

"And they're grateful?" she persisted. "Grateful enough to let you stay in their best suite?"

"Yes."

His tone warned that the discussion had come to an end. She stewed over the implications, aware that she was missing something, something important. Perhaps if she weren't so distracted by him, she'd have figured out what it was. Pouring the coffee, he filled a single plate with fresh fruit and croissants. One plate, she noticed, not two. Apparently, they were meant to share, if his placement of it between their coffee mugs was any indication.

The nook was small and intimate, becoming far smaller and more intimate the instant Harry joined her. Or maybe it just felt that way because he took up more than his fair share of the space. He reached for a croissant and ripped it in half and Madison closed her eyes, fighting a reaction she had no business experiencing. It had to be lust, or something equally earthy and impractical. Here it was, nine in the morning, but it might as well have been late at night, after an evening of wine, music and blatant seduction. It took a full minute before she trusted herself enough to reach for her coffee cup without betraying the confusing jumble of emotions.

A long swallow sent caffeine shooting through her veins. Maybe the coffee had been a mistake. Caffeine only aggravated the situation, making her tension more pronounced. A strawberry didn't help, nor did eating the half a croissant Harry had left on the plate. In fact, that only made it worse. Each bite was a vivid reminder of his hands shredding the flaky bread. He had distinctive hands—large, long-fingered, broad-palmed hands—capable of covering a lot of territory with very little effort. She'd discovered that much in the elevator. Or perhaps her attack of nerves had something to do with the watchful gleam in his hazel eyes. It was as though he knew precisely what she was experiencing. Knew and was amused by it.

"Stop it."

He lifted an eyebrow. "Stop what?"

"I don't know what love principle you're practicing on me, but cut it out. I'm not into those sorts of games."

"I don't play games."

She shoved the plate in his direction. "You're trying to seduce me. Don't bother to deny it. I can tell when I'm being seduced and you, my friend, have some hot and heavy love vibe going on. I don't know if it's a trick your father taught you or if you came up with this one all on your own. But knock it off, I'm not interested.''

He picked up a huge dark red strawberry and bit deeply into the juicy flesh. ''Love vibe.''

''Don't pretend innocence. You don't do it well.'' She waved her hand to encompass everything from his sexy eyes, to his sexy strawberry-flavored mouth, to his sexy juice-stained fingers. ''Turn it off so we can get down to business.''

Harry regarded her with interest. ''How do you propose I do that?''

''No switch?'' she demanded.

He shrugged apologetically. ''None that I've been able to find.''

''Then how about if you pretend we're in a business meeting. You can make that sort of adjustment, can't you?''

''It'll be tough.'' He gestured downward. ''I'm not wearing a suit.''

''Yeah, I noticed.'' Boy, had she noticed! ''Maybe that's part of the trouble. Come on, Harry. This is important to me.''

Just like that he went from seducer to business exec. ''Talk to me.''

It was the same phrase she used when dealing with her family and she acknowledged the connection with a fleeting smile. ''We have a problem.'' A far worse one than she'd first suspected considering her uncontrollable reaction to him, but she'd have to deal with that some other time. ''I'm sure you don't want your father involved in an unfortunate relationship any more than I want my grandmother involved in one.''

''Wrong.''

She stared in disbelief. "You don't care if they rush into an unhappy marriage?"

"No, I mean it's not my problem. It's not yours, either. If they rush into marriage, they'll have to deal with the consequences. I repeat. It's none of our business."

"So you aren't willing to help?"

He eyed her warily. "What do you mean, help? You're not going to interfere in their affair, Madison. I won't let you."

She folded her arms across her chest and glared at him. "He may be your father, Harry. But he's a *love* expert." Didn't he understand the significance of that? "Sunny doesn't stand a chance against him. And now that I've had personal experience with the sort of techniques he's likely to employ—thanks to you, I might add—I'm even more concerned about my grandmother."

"I don't employ techniques. And my father isn't a love expert. He's simply touting a book about love. If you'd just read the damn thing—"

"What if he's using Sunny as a model in order to write a sequel?" Madison smiled triumphantly at Harry's stunned expression. "You hadn't thought about that, had you? Sunny could be some sort of experiment."

"He's not going to marry an experiment."

"He might if it meant another blockbuster book."

"You're being ridiculous." Harry shoved back his chair. For some reason, the extra space didn't allow her to breathe any easier, perhaps because of the anger that turned his eyes from an autumnal hazel to a sandstorm brown. "This is my father you're talking about and I'm starting to get ticked off at the assumptions you're making about him. Totally unsubstantiated assumptions, I might add.''

''I understand. You're feeling protective. Well, I am, too. So here's what I suggest.''

He forked his hand through his hair. ''I'm not going to like this, am I?''

''Probably not.'' Not that his opinion would stop her. ''I want to *monitor* their engagement.''

Sure enough, he didn't appreciate her suggestion one little bit. He also took an inordinate amount of time before responding. Finally, he said, ''In that case you've left me no alternative.''

Uh-oh. ''I'm not going to like this, am I?'' she asked, echoing his words.

He didn't pull his punches. ''Not even a little. I'm going to *monitor* you monitoring them.'' He touched a berry-stained fingertip to her mouth, stopping her before she could voice a single word of complaint. ''That's not open to negotiation, Madison. Either you agree or I'll tell them what you're up to.''

''That's blackmail!'' she argued around his finger.

His hand lingered for an instant longer before falling away. ''And monitoring is just a polite word for spying.'' He waited for that to sink in. ''I suggest you tell me what's first on the agenda before I come to my senses and put an end to this nonsense.''

She fought against the insidious pull of his touch. The temptation to wrap herself around him and kiss his strawberry-flavored mouth was almost more than she could stand. ''The picnic, remember? I have Rosy tracking down the happy couple as we speak. As soon as she finds out where they're headed, we'll follow.''

He sighed. ''You gave me the impression we'd been

invited to join them on this picnic. We haven't been, have we?"

"Not exactly."

"You mean, not at all."

Why did he look at her as though she were one of his more disappointing economic models? It made her feel like a set of confused equations in need of serious alteration. She didn't care for the sensation at all. Their situation wasn't just about business. Family resided at its core. "You don't understand, Harry. I'm responsible for my grandmother."

"She's old enough to be responsible for herself."

"She's only known your father for two days."

"They've known each other for a year."

"E-mails. Phone calls." She dismissed their relationship with a wave of her hand. "That's not knowing each other. Not well enough for marriage."

He studied her for several tension-filled minutes. "Why is this bothering you so much? What's going on, Madison?"

"I've already explained. I'm responsible. Sunny and I have always looked out for each other."

"You don't think she's capable of looking out for herself?"

"To a certain extent. But if Sunny has one great failing, it's that she's controlled by her emotions. That's why we make such a great team."

"You're the brains and she's the heart."

Did he have to sound so amused? She lifted her chin. "Something like that."

"I promise you, Madison. My father isn't going to do anything to hurt her. And I'm not going to let you ruin my father's happiness just because you have trust issues."

She stared blankly. "Trust issues?"

"It's the only thing I can figure. Otherwise you'd be celebrating Sunny's good fortune instead of trying to put an end to it."

Madison swept to her feet. "I have no idea what you're talking about."

"Now there's a surprise."

He climbed to his feet, as well. Without her high heels, he towered over her even more than yesterday and she rushed into speech to prevent his expanding on any more inane theories. "Here's the plan... We'll keep a discreet distance between us. But I want to make sure that Sunny isn't being blinded by love principles."

"You'll be able to spot any he might use on her, I assume?"

Now came the tricky part. "With your help."

Amusement returned the brilliance to his eyes. "So I'm supposed to warn you if he's using a page out of the book, so to speak."

"Exactly."

"Let me get this straight. The other Sunflowers are *more* impractical than you?"

"Very funny." She turned and walked briskly from the kitchen. "Let's move, Harry. If we're going on a picnic we have to get organized."

"Are you sure you can afford this much time away from work? Won't there be other Sunflowers clamoring for your attention?"

"I'll have my cell phone with me. Rosy will call if anything urgent crops up."

He looked briefly intrigued. "Does that happen often?"

"Every day." Opening the door to his suite, she swept

through. "What you don't seem to realize is that the Sunflowers need me."

"I think you have it backward, sweetheart," he muttered. "I'm beginning to suspect that you need them."

CHAPTER FIVE

Principle 5: View the one you love
in every possible light.
True love never fades nor wilts—not even
beneath the harshest conditions...

IT BEGAN as one of those rare Seattle days, with craggy mountains standing in stunning relief against a violently blue sky. The Puget Sound could be mistaken for a sheet of glass, dotted with sailboats and mirroring the Olympic Mountain range. Not that it would stay that way for long, Harry acknowledged. Already heavy, black clouds were gathering to the west, rolling toward them with impressive speed.

But for now the freshly mowed grass smelled sweeter than grass had a right to smell. Even their alcove in the park could be considered a romantic paradise, flowers blooming in brilliant profusion, bushes screening them from curious onlookers. It was sheer perfection—a man, a woman, food, a comfortable blanket. And then there was the view...

Harry shook his head. The view was one of the most glorious he'd ever seen, if somewhat dissatisfying. Madison knelt in the grass, her nose stuck in a laurel bush. Peering through the thick green leaves at Sunny and his father, her pert backside waggled in his direction. As an average, lusty, red-blooded male, he appreciated such an impressive vista. But right now he'd have preferred looking at flashing dark eyes and cheeks flushed with enthusiasm rather than the sort covered by the skirt of her red sundress.

Yesterday, after their run-in with the elevator, he'd found her delectable as the consummate businesswoman. Last night in the restaurant she'd been a flame of gold that tempted his touch beyond endurance even as she threatened to burn his hand. But dressed in glowing red, flimsy bits of sandals strapped to her feet and her hair in casual disarray, she'd become sheer fantasy. A mild breeze played with the dark strands, lifting them around her face before tossing them in a swirl of abandoned waves. She shoved the curls out of her way with an annoyed mutter.

The trick to it, Harry decided, was to get Madison's focus off Sunny and Bartholomew and on to him. Considering her powers of concentration that would prove quite a feat. But all modesty aside, he was up to the task. After all, he'd diverted the focus of some of the most aggressive men in corporate America. How tough could one determined brunette be?

"The salmon is fresh," he thought to mention.

"I would hope so." Her backside wriggled some more as she changed position. "After all, this is Seattle."

"The cheese and bread are local, too."

"Uh-huh." She flipped her hand in a wave that gave him permission to dig in. "Darn it all, those people are blocking my line of sight. What the heck are they looking at that's worth all the fuss?"

"The view? I know I'm giving it my full attention." What else did he have to do? He rested on his elbows and released his breath in a sigh. "I have a recommendation for next time you go on a covert mission."

Wiggle. Waggle. Wiggle. "Don't be ridiculous."
Swish-hitch-wriggle. "This isn't a covert mission."

He clamped his back teeth on a groan. It took a whole
two minutes before he could gather his control enough
to reply. Perhaps a determined brunette would prove
more of a challenge than he'd anticipated. "Anything
that involves peering through bushes at unsuspecting in-
nocents can be termed covert. I suggest you wear clothing in a color that blends in with your surroundings.
You're a little hard to miss in that outfit."

"Good suggestion," she approved. "I'll make a note
of it."

This was ridiculous. Time to put an end to it.
"Madison, your grandmother and my father aren't going
anywhere. Have a bite to eat and give them some privacy."

"Hang on. Those people have finally moved. And
about time, too." She inhaled sharply. "Harry! Your
father's doing something to Sunny. Come here and take
a look."

"Is he strangling her, perhaps?"

"No." Madison swung around. "Whatever gave you
that idea?"

"It was just a passing thought. I can't imagine why
it occurred to me."

"Neither can I." She eyed him in concern. "Is there
some risk that he might actually do that? There isn't a
history of abuse in your family, is there?"

"Not yet."

"Good." She maneuvered on all fours to another
bush. Shoving aside the branches of a rhododendron, she
returned her attention to the couple at the far end of the
park. "Come look at this, Harry. Is that a principle he's
using?"

His anger tended to be slow to ignite. But Madison had the uncanny knack of heaping dry kindling on sensitive subjects. He took a deep breath and struggled to utilize the sage advice he'd offered countless times to feuding board members. For some strange reason he couldn't recall a single word. "Honey, if you'd read the damned book, you'd know that isn't how the principles work. They aren't techniques like...like sexual positions or something. They're simply commonsense rules for forming a strong, loving relationship."

She snorted. "Yeah, right. You can't fool me with that one, Harry."

"I repeat. If you'd read the book—"

"I can't. I lost it on the elevator."

"I'll get you another one."

"Don't bother. I skimmed some of the choicer parts. Take another peek at Chapter Three and tell me again it's not about sex. All that stuff about touching and smelling and looking. No wonder Sunny's so bamboozled."

"Chapter One is looking. Chapter Two is listening. Chapter Three references touch, taste and scent. Don't you think appealing to all the senses is an important part of an initial romantic attraction?"

She started to reply, then hesitated. An instant later, her spine snapped into a rigid line and she swiveled to face him. Her gathering frown bore an unfortunate similarity to the threatening clouds filling the western sky and bearing down on them with rumbling determination. "I just thought of something."

Finally. He'd captured her attention. Though judging by her frown, he may regret succeeding. "What's that, sweetheart?"

"Chapters one through three."

"What about them?"

"You've read them, right?"

"I'm familiar with the entire book. What's your point?"

"I'm talking about on the elevator." She pinned him with a stare rapidly filling with feminine outrage. "Was it deliberate?"

"You've lost me."

"Then let me make it perfectly clear." She planted her hands on her hips. "Did you or did you not hustle me through those first three principles? On purpose, I mean."

At least her attention was on him again, if he could only find a way to keep it there. "Hustle is such a negative word."

"I'm serious, Harry."

A wariness had darkened her eyes, suspicion and distrust eclipsing every other emotion. He didn't care for the expression, suspecting her reaction had its origins in circumstances and events from her past. Time to defuse the situation. "We discussed this after we got off the elevator. I told you we'd managed to work our way through the first three principles."

"*Accidently.* I'm talking about a deliberate attempt on your part to seduce me using that book."

He answered with absolute honesty. "As tempting as that sounds, it didn't even occur to me."

"Then how did we manage to work our way through so many of your father's precious principles in such a short period of time?"

They were definitely dealing with issues from her past, Harry decided, issues connected to trust problems. None of which boded well for future discussions—especially considering all he'd kept from her. Hell. He should have been honest from the start. He would have been, too, if not for Sunny and his father. He thrust a hand through his hair. It was a little late to explain everything now, but with luck he'd have an opportunity to redress those errors in judgment as they arose. In the meantime, he'd do what he could to reassure her about the hours they'd spent together on the elevator. And then he'd try his damnedest to uncover the truth about her past and help heal the wounds that made her so vulnerable.

"Think about it, Madison. It's literally impossible for two people to be alone together for hours on end and not have them react to each other through at least one of the senses. We talked to each other. That's one right there."

"We touched."

He couldn't help grinning. "I remember."

"This isn't funny." She sat on the blanket, facing him, and folded her arms across her chest in a defensive posture. The sunlight caught in her hair and spilled across her shoulders in a stream of liquid gold. If it weren't for the alarm and anger blazing in her eyes, he'd have tugged her into his arms and given her a hands-on reminder of all they'd experienced on the elevator. "Tell me whether you were deliberately pulling some sort of principle stuff on me."

"I admit there was some serious masculine chemistry going on."

"I knew it!"

"If it makes you feel any better, your female chemistry was in full flower, too." Her mouth compressed at the suggestion, warning that any discussion regarding her flowering chemistry wouldn't make her feel any better. But he refused to let her off the hook. Whether she liked it or not, her hormones had been in as much of an uproar as his, and he wasn't about to pretend otherwise. "Was our interaction on the elevator a setup? No way. Was I sneaking you through the principles? Not a chance."

"How can I be sure?"

She'd tossed more kindling on his temper and it promptly ignited. Shoving plastic ware out of his way, he leaned closer. "If I start using principles on you, there won't be any doubt in your mind about what I'm doing."

Her eyes widened. "What do you mean?"

"It seems to me that you're not going to be satisfied until you get a sample to use for comparison. Maybe if I give you a personal demonstration of all the principles you'll know what Sunny can expect."

"No, I—"

He didn't give her time to say another word. Tipping her back onto the blanket, he came down on top of her and thrust his hands deep into her curls. "Look at me, Madison. What do you see?"

She swallowed. "A very determined man. Maybe even an annoyed one."

"Wrong. You see a hungry man. And I see the perfect woman to satisfy that hunger." He whispered a heated proposition in her ear. "And what do you hear?"

She shuddered in his arms. "A suggestion. I hear a most interesting suggestion."

"That's right. Only it's more than a suggestion. It's a promise I intend to keep at our earliest convenience."

He bent his head to nuzzle the joining of her shoulder and neck, thrusting the strap of her sundress out of his way. A slight movement on the other side of the bushes caught his attention. Sunny peered through the branches

and waved gaily. Next to her Bartholomew regarded his
son with a broad, amused grin. Harry choked.

"Is something wrong?" Madison asked.

He motioned frantically for their audience to get lost.
Fortunately, they took the hint and trotted off in the direction of the parking lot. "Not a thing, sweetheart. Now
where was I?"

"Explaining the principles to me," she replied a little
too fast. She must have thought so, as well, since she
immediately infused a note of righteous indignation into
her voice. "Explaining them against my will, I might
add."

He buried a smile. "Sorry, my sweet. But you're getting a lesson in the principles, whether you want one or
not."

"Just so you know I'm opposed to the entire experiment." She trotted out the lie without a hint of shame.
"Totally opposed."

"Objection noted. Where were we?"

"We'd just finished sight and hearing. You'd made a
most improper suggestion involving the two of us, a
scandalous lack of clothing, a bed, some champagne and
strawberries and topping various parts of my anatomy
with scoops of ice cream," she reminded with alacrity.
"And I was shocked speechless. Now, what's next?"

Oh, yeah. The ice cream. How could that have slipped
his mind? He fought for coherent thought, finally seizing
on one of the three senses that he'd somehow forgotten.
Who'd have imagined one over-controlling, obsessive,
practical-minded woman could have such an affect on
him? "Did you know that when we were on the elevator
it was your voice and your scent that helped form my
first impressions of you? Every so often I caught the

faintest hint of your perfume, and something else. Something that's unique to you.''

Her eyes fluttered closed and she inhaled deeply, smiling in pleasure. "So is yours. It reminds me of a cleansing rainstorm.''

She wasn't far wrong. He shifted so she wouldn't detect the first warning spattering of raindrops and pressed her hands tight against his chest. "Sight, hearing, scent…and now touch. What do you feel, Madison?''

"Your heart.''

"Beating in rhythm with yours.'' He brushed a kiss across her mouth, their lips barely touching. Then another, slightly deeper. Then a third that warned of a passion held barely in check. Her mouth blossomed beneath his, welcoming him. He swept inward, sparking something hot and primitive and desperate. "And last, but far from least, what do you taste, Madison? Tell me.''

Her response came as a slow sigh of want. "You.''

"Isn't this how it should be? Doesn't this feel right? Now do you understand how the principles are supposed to work?''

Her eyes slowly flickered open, like someone waking from a deep, delicious dream. "Oh, yes! It feels—'' Her brows drew together. "Harry? Why…why is your hair wet?''

"There's an excellent explanation for that.''

"Oh, good heavens. It's raining. Harry!'' She shoved at his shoulders. "Get up. You're getting soaked. Why didn't you tell me?''

Reluctantly, he rolled off her. So much for giving her a firsthand demonstration of the principles of love. With swift efficiency, he dumped the remains of their picnic into the basket. The light rain intensified, within seconds becoming a downpour. Tossing the blanket over

Madison's head, he snatched up the picnic basket with one hand and grabbed her with the other. They ran for the car. Unfortunately, Madison's sandals weren't made with a Seattle rainstorm in mind. They hadn't gone more than ten feet before they tripped her up.

"Screw it." Harry tossed down the basket, ripped the blanket off her head and pulled her into his arms.

Rain pounded down on top of them, but in that moment he didn't give a damn. Lifting her against him, he kissed her. There was something intensely primitive about kissing a woman in the pouring rain, their bodies locked together, their skin slick, the heat of their want a striking counterpoint to the chill of the air. All he could think about was peeling away her clothes and laying her down in the wet, fragrant grass and making her his. His desire drove him beyond rational consideration, his need the most desperate he'd ever felt. The rain washed away all civilized thought, the unrelenting rhythm echoing the raw passion throbbing through his veins.

She clung to him, her soaked sundress sealed to his cotton shirt, her skirt twining around his legs in a loving embrace. It was as though every part of her had become joined to him. He swept his hands down her back, unable to resist exploring. She was round where a woman should be rounded—full, generous breasts, hips that curved into a lush bottom that filled his hands, well-formed thighs made to wrap around a man and cradle him close. With each stroking caress, she shivered with unmistakable urgency, pulling back only long enough to utter two delicious words.

"Don't stop."

He wasn't a man who took orders well. But he made an exception this once, losing all sense of time and place. He wanted the woman in his arms, was driven by the compulsion to brand her in the most elemental of ways. He'd spent years fighting to control the baser side of his nature. But not here. Not now. Resistance proved impossible. He dragged the straps of her sundress downward at the same instant a faint, outraged squawk sounded nearby. At first Harry thought Madison had changed her mind and was voicing a reluctant protest. Then he realized it came from her purse. He swore beneath his breath.

"It's my phone," she murmured apologetically.

"It sounds like someone's torturing it." Or maybe it was just wishful thinking on his part.

She took a step backward, clutching her gaping dress to her chest. "I think the rain killed it."

"What a shame."

"There's no need for sarcasm." It would seem that sanity had returned with a vengeance, the rain dousing any hint of flame or fire. Judging by her expression all that remained was a heap of soggy ashes. She glanced over her shoulder at the picnic area. "Everyone's left."

Reluctantly he adjusted the straps of her sundress. Not that it helped much. The rain had drenched the shape from the garment, the weight of the water dragging it downward in the most interesting places. Her breasts glistened beneath the cleansing rinse and he gave in to temptation, sweeping the moisture from the rounded slopes. She didn't protest his actions—nor did she encourage them. Reluctantly he released her. There would be other opportunities, Harry reminded himself. No point in forcing the issue.

"Yes, everyone's left," he confirmed. "Apparently the other picnickers don't like kissing in the rain as much as we do."

She looked around, shivering. "Sunny and Bartholomew? Where are they?"

He shrugged. "Long gone, I would imagine. I doubt they lingered once it began to rain."

He'd said the wrong thing. Alarm flickered across her face. "Oh, no. This is terrible. Do you think they saw us?"

"Terrible?" Not even the chill of the rain could cool his flash of anger. "You mind telling me what's so terrible about it?"

She avoided his gaze. "If they saw us, it'll give them the wrong idea."

"Funny. I thought it might give them the right idea."

"We were just trying out a few of the rules." She backed another step away from him, her actions speaking far louder than her words. "That's *all*. It was nothing personal."

"Keep telling yourself that." He swept the blanket from the grass. "If you're into self-delusion, you might even be able to sound convincing."

"You can't believe it was more than that."

He didn't bother arguing. Crouching, he stripped away the shreds of her sandals and tossed them aside. He considered snatching her into his arms and carrying her across the grass to the parking lot. One glimpse of the tense set of her mouth and the wariness building in her eyes changed his mind. He limited himself to catching her hand in his and resuming the trek to the car. The rain didn't feel primitive and seductive anymore. It felt cold and wet and uncomfortable. He unlocked the car and held the door for her. Her dress clung, showing off a figure her business suit had only hinted at. Even the gold dress hadn't done her full justice. There was something about wet red cotton pasted to a near-naked body that appealed beyond belief.

His annoyance dissipated. Patience, he reminded himself. He couldn't expect to overcome twenty-five years' worth of carefully forged barriers in just a few days. "Let's get you home so you can change."

"Thanks. I'd appreciate that." She wrapped her arms around herself. "I'm freezing."

"I'll turn the heater on. It should warm you up in no time."

The instant they were belted into their seats, she gave him directions to Magnolia, a residential area on the outskirts of the city. Her home sat on a bluff with an impressive view of the Sound, and was a sprawling two-story affair that looked like it had belonged to the same family for generations. She hesitated before exiting the car.

"Would you like to come in and dry off?"

"Yes." He smiled at the conflicting emotions that slipped across her face—anticipation, wariness, nervous hesitation combined with a hint of renewed passion. "But I'm not going to."

"Why?" The question was a mere whisper, part query, part complaint.

"Because I'd want to pick up where we left off in the park."

She turned abruptly, staring through the front windshield. "Would that be so bad?"

"No. I think it would be very good." Incredible, if he was any judge. "But there are still a lot of issues standing between us. Issues that need to be resolved before we take this any further."

"You mean the book, and Sunny and Bartholomew."

"It's more than that, I'm afraid."

Her jaw tightened. "If you're referring to my job—"

"That's part of it. There's also my job."

Comprehension dawned along with a hint of guilt. "I remember you mentioned that this was a working vacation. I've kept you from work, haven't I?"

"Yes." But not the way she meant. "And until I've completed this latest assignment it wouldn't be appropriate to begin an affair with you."

Her lashes flickered in reaction and she slanted him a quick glance. "An affair seems a bit…precipitous. We haven't known each other for very long."

"I agree." His mouth twisted. "That doesn't seem to stop us, does it?"

He saw the denial building in her expressive eyes. Then her breath released on a sigh of surrender and she shook her head. "It doesn't make any sense, does it?"

His laugh held a hint of irony. "I think it makes perfect sense. We're attracted to each other. I just don't understand why you're so determined to fight the idea." He took a wild guess. "Are you worried about commitment?"

She didn't duck the question as he'd expected. "That's part of it."

Now they were getting somewhere. He'd try taking it one step further and see what happened. "Are you afraid to commit? Or afraid I won't?"

"Both." She fumbled for her purse and reached for the car door handle, distancing herself from him physically as well as emotionally. "I have to go."

He reached out to stop her. "Madison—"

She threw him a quick, wary look over her shoulder. "I'm afraid of how vulnerable it would make me. Does that answer your question?"

"Yes. It also raises a number of others. Why do you think commitment makes you vulnerable?"

"Because I watched what committing to a man did to my mother."

She opened the door and escaped the car. Her hair had begun to dry, springing about her face in a dark halo of ringlets, but the rain remained unrelenting, dragging the spontaneity from the carefree curls. He thrust open the driver's door and went after her. He was soaked again in seconds. Not that he gave a damn.

"What happened to your mother?" He had to raise his voice to be heard over the unceasing thrum of the rain. "Why does a commitment make you vulnerable?"

She turned and ran barefoot toward her front porch. She'd only ascended the first two risers before facing him. She was as drenched as he was, her once-perky dress the only splash of color in a world washed gray and dismal. The brilliant red had faded to a pale imitation of its former glory and clung in shapeless folds. Worse, her expression reflected the vulnerability she feared so much. More than anything he wanted to gather her close and offer the sort of comfort she'd no doubt reject.

"Madison, answer my question. What happened to your mother?"

He sensed it was sheer pride that kept her standing on the steps, a stubborn refusal to give in to the temptation of either tears or flight. "She loved my father." Madison's hands clenched at her sides as she fought for control. "She committed herself to him, every bit of herself."

"And their marriage fell apart?" It couldn't be that simple.

Play the
"LAS VEGAS"
GAME

GET
3 FREE
GIFTS!

FREE
GIFTS!

FREE
GIFTS!

FREE
GIFTS!

TURN THE PAGE TO PLAY! Details inside!

Play the "LAS VEGAS" Game and get 3 FREE GIFTS!

FREE GIFTS!

FREE GIFTS!

1. Pull back all 3 tabs on the card at right. Then check the claim chart to see what we have for you — 2 FREE BOOKS and a gift — ALL YOURS! A FREE!

2. Send back this card and you'll receive brand-new Harlequin Romance® novels. These books have a cover price of $3.50 each in the U.S. and $3.99 each in Canada, but they are yours to keep absolutely free.

3. There's no catch. You're under no obligation to buy anything. We char nothing — ZERO — for your first shipment. And you don't have to ma any minimum number of purchases — not even one!

4. The fact is, thousands of readers enjoy receiving their books by mail fro the Harlequin Reader Service®. They enjoy the convenience of home delivery...they like getting the best new novels at discount prices, BEFOR they're available in stores...and they love their *Heart to Heart* newslette featuring author news, horoscopes, recipes, book reviews and much mo

5. We hope that after receiving your free books you'll want to remain a subscriber. But the choice is yours — to continue or cancel, any time all! So why not take us up on our invitation, with no risk of any kind. You'll be glad you did!

Visit us online at
www.eHarlequin.com

FREE!
No Obligation to Buy!
No Purchase Necessary!

Play the
"LAS VEGAS" Game

> **PEEL BACK HERE** ▶
> **PEEL BACK HERE** ▶
> **PEEL BACK HERE** ▶

YES! I have pulled back the 3 tabs. Please send me all the free Harlequin Romance® books and the gift for which I qualify. I understand that I am under no obligation to purchase any books, as explained on the back and opposite page.

386 HDL DC4R

186 HDL DC4H
(H-R-OS-05/01)

NAME (PLEASE PRINT CLEARLY)

ADDRESS

APT.# CITY

STATE/PROV. ZIP/POSTAL CODE

7	7	7	**GET 2 FREE BOOKS & A FREE MYSTERY GIFT!**
🍀	🍀	🍀	**GET 2 FREE BOOKS!**
🍒	🍒	🍒	**GET 1 FREE BOOK!**
🔔	🔔	🔔	**TRY AGAIN!**

Offer limited to one per household and not valid to current Harlequin Romance® subscribers. All orders subject to approval.

BUSINESS REPLY MAIL

FIRST-CLASS MAIL   PERMIT NO. 717   BUFFALO, NY

POSTAGE WILL BE PAID BY ADDRESSEE

HARLEQUIN READER SERVICE
3010 WALDEN AVE
PO BOX 1867
BUFFALO NY 14240-9952

NO POSTAGE
NECESSARY
IF MAILED
IN THE
UNITED STATES

"It did more than fall apart. It was taken apart piece by piece until there was nothing left of my mother."

He pushed harder, sensing he wouldn't be given another opportunity to learn about her past anytime soon. "What happened, sweetheart? Who took the marriage apart?"

"My father!" she shouted, her anger punching a hole in her protective barriers. "My practical, logical, accountant father. He promised to take care of my mother. And instead he destroyed her. I don't want that to happen to me. I don't want a practical, logical man in my life. I don't want a man who can take apart my life with such deliberate precision."

"I'd never do that!"

Heaven continued to unleash its torrent of rain, a gray curtain of water dropping between them, separating them, covering them, parting them. It was nature at its most elemental, pelting with unrelenting force onto their heads and shoulders. Madison crept backward up the steps toward the porch.

"You won't hurt me because I won't let you," she called over the pounding of the rain.

"Sweetheart—"

"I have to go. One of the Sunflowers phoned while we were at the park. Someone needs me."

I need you, he almost said. "Okay, fine. I'll see you tomorrow at your office. We'll continue our discussion then."

His gamble paid off and she nodded, though her eyes remained filled with darkness. "Nine o'clock, Jones. And we'll *finish* our discussion then."

He wouldn't let her get away with that one. "We're a long way from finishing anything. We'll continue our discussion then, not finish it."

Her mouth twisted into a parody of a smile. "We'll see."

She disappeared into the house and Harry stood on the walkway staring at the tightly closed door. "You're not going to stay closed for long, sweetheart. I intend to see to that, personally. And that's a promise."

"So which rule are you going to demonstrate for Madison?" Aunt Dell asked her nephew. "I just can't decide. I want to pick a special one, since she's so special. But I can't figure out which one that would be. How did you decide?"

Harley grinned. "Easy. I'm gonna draw a rule out of a hat."

"Very scientific," she approved. "Maybe we should suggest that method to Sunny for the rest of us, especially with so many rules to choose from."

"You can do that right after I get mine out of the way." He shoved his hand into a Mariners' baseball cap and pulled out a scrap of paper. "The way I've got it figured, the sooner we trot Madison through the rules, the sooner I get my Beemer."

"A BMW?" Aunt Dell's brow wrinkled in confusion. "But, I thought you were after a Mercedes."

"Changed my mind." He opened the paper and read it through. "Okay, this'll be no sweat."

She peered over Harley's shoulder. "Which one is it?"

"It says something about working together and talking." He laughed. "Man did I luck out. Talking is all Madison ever does. So all I have to do is get them working together and let her yak his ear off and that little red sports job is all mine."

"Dearest? I'm not sure that's quite what the rule means."

He waved Aunt Dell's uncertainty aside. "Relax. I've got it covered. I'm so positive this'll work that Sunny can book the church on my matchmaking scheme alone. And why?" He slapped the cap on his head and grinned, bits of paper raining down around his ears. "Because Harley Sunflower, love expert, is in charge. That's why."

"Yes, dear," Aunt Dell murmured. "In the meantime, the rest of us will hope your rule isn't one of the more important ones."

CHAPTER SIX

Principle 6: How to Work Together as Partners...
Finances, Children, and other Important Discussions.

"OKAY, I'm here," Madison announced the minute Harry opened his hotel room door. She strove to keep her tone direct and to the point, without a hint of the emotional turbulence from their last encounter. In an act of sheer defiance, she'd even worn a brilliant red business suit the exact shade of yesterday's sundress. "What's the big emergency?"

Harry released his breath in a long, exasperated sigh. "And good morning to you, too."

"Oh, dear. I've done it again, haven't I?" When would she learn? Perhaps if she hadn't been trying to pretend yesterday had never happened, she'd have remembered to utilize an ounce of common courtesy. "Good morning, Harry. How are you?"

"Fine, thanks." He swung the door to his hotel room open in an exact imitation of the previous morning, though this time there was a knowing expression in his gaze—an acknowledgment of both the color she'd worn and the reason behind it. "Won't you come in?"

Pasting a gracious smile on her face, she stepped across the threshold and turned to confront him. "So what's the big— Oh, good *heavens!*"

Every thought in her head evaporated as she got her first good look at him. He stood leaning against his hotel

100

door, the very picture of indolent masculine grace. Gone was the formal suit and tie he'd worn on previous occasions. Gone, as well, were the jeans and casual shirt. The neatly combed hair of a practical-minded economist had also vanished, along with every other guise of civilization. All that remained was a dangerous smile and a low-slung towel.

He folded his arms, drawing her attention to impressive biceps and an immense expanse of muscular everything—chest, arms, shoulders. How on earth had he stuffed all that into a suit jacket? It didn't seem possible. Swirls of dark brown hair formed a perfect, rippled triangle across his chest and her gaze followed a thin rivulet of hair draining out of the bottom of the inverted pyramid. It trickled down his flat belly before disappearing into the towel and she had the craziest urge to follow that seductive path and see where it led. If it weren't for the fact that the towel appeared to hang on his lean hips through sheer will alone, she might have turned thought to action.

Harry shifted his stance and the towel hitched downward another threatening inch. "When you focus your attention on something, you give it your full attention, don't you?"

"Yes, I do," she responded absently. "I have excellent powers of concentration."

"So I've noticed. May I suggest you shift that concentration elsewhere? Otherwise *my* attention will be focused on how quickly I can get you out of your clothes and into the nearest bed."

Madison jerked her gaze upward. "What?"

He unfolded from his stance and approached. Somehow he managed to coerce all those muscles into working together in perfect coordination, each bunching and releasing in a fluid series of dips and swells. The sheer symmetry fascinated her. In that moment, she'd have given anything to have Harry spend the next couple hours in constant movement so she could analyze the amazing play of tendon and sinew. She wanted to learn his unique rhythm, to imprint and match it to her own.

Of course, in order to do full justice to her analysis, she'd have to insist the towel go, as well. Yes, indeed. She'd definitely have to make a few alterations to her blueprint of the perfect man. Somehow she'd forgotten to include all of—she examined Harry a little closer—*this*…this lovely masculine magnificence. It was an oversight she'd make a point of correcting at her earliest opportunity.

Harry snagged her chin with his index finger, forcing her gaze upward. "Talk fast or you won't be able to say anything for a long, long time."

"I won't?" A fierce green light sparked in his eyes, affecting Madison's breathing in the oddest way. Or maybe it had something to do with being so close to all those impressive tendons and sinews. "Why not?"

"Because my mouth will be in the way."

Just like that, she flashed back on their rain-sweetened kiss from the previous day. She liked having his mouth in the way. Liked it too much. His kisses had the unique ability to untangle knots she'd spent a lifetime tying. And then, right when she thought every last one had come undone, new knots formed, the sort that made her acutely aware of the vulnerability that came from being a woman in the arms of a man she found irresistible.

The main problem with their kiss had been the aftermath. She'd been so close to surrendering to Harry. Even when he'd left, it had taken hours to scrape together a pinch of common sense about how to handle the situation—the sort of common sense that would keep her out of his bed. But stay out of it she would. She couldn't risk the consequences if she allowed him to overrun her defenses. He'd already gotten too close to places she guarded with painstaking care, allowing him to catch a glimpse of aspects of her life that she preferred to keep buried. She couldn't afford to reveal any further vulnerabilities.

She fought to infuse a business-like note in her voice with only limited success. "I didn't come here so you could kiss me." Despite what she might want.

"But that's what you'll get. Tell me why you're here, sweetheart. Otherwise I'm going to make good on my promise."

She puzzled over that. "Don't you know?"

"Uh-huh." He reached for his towel with pointed intent.

"Wait a minute!" She took a hasty step backward. "Maybe you should put on some clothes. I think it might help our discussion." It would certainly help her end of the discussion.

"I have a better idea. Why don't you shed a few?"

She shook her head with what she prayed was sufficient resolution. "I'd rather not."

A brief debate waged in his eyes. Then he shrugged the shoulders she'd embarrassed herself by drooling all over. "Give me a few minutes to shower and dress. After that we'll talk."

"About business."

He simply smiled. "Among other things."

She watched him walk away with a growing feeling of unease. That's what she was afraid of. She didn't want to talk about the picnic or what happened afterward. He'd start asking questions about her background. About her mother and father and those terrible years when they'd divorced. And then he'd find out just how much of an Adams she really was. There were facts about herself she preferred to keep hidden in the darkest recesses of her soul—facts she hadn't even told her family. Facts Harry threatened to pry loose.

The faint sound of running water distracted her, escaping from behind closed doors. She wished she couldn't hear it. The mere thought of Harry in a shower cubicle was enough to cause her far-too-analytical brain to short circuit. A delectable image of him popped into her head—Harry, stripped naked, streams of water surging in and out of all his various bulges and creases. He'd take up a whole lot of room in that shower. Why, if she were to join him, she'd be squashed tight as a bug between him and the tiled stall, their bodies, slick with soap slipping and sliding—

Harry snapped his fingers in front of her face. "Wake up, princess."

The tantalizing image burst like a soap bubble and she stared at the fully showered, shaved and dressed Harry standing in front of her. "What? You're finished *already?*" Where had the time gone? She could have sworn only a scant minute or two had passed.

"Yes, I'm finished already. And you're doing it again."

She couldn't seem to wrap her brain around his words. "Doing what again?"

He leaned in. "You're looking at me in a way that makes me think I can get out of my clothes a hell of a lot faster than I got into them."

"I'm just surprised that you managed to get so much done in such a short amount of time," she muttered.

"I've been gone almost twenty minutes." His eyes

glittered with far too much awareness. "You didn't realize it had been that long?"

She shrugged, snagging the first excuse that drifted through her head. "Blame it on work. I was considering the wisdom of whether to add more tech stocks to my portfolio or sell short on Biogenetics."

"Are you asking my advice?"

"That won't be necessary." Excellent. She'd said all that without a hint of drool. "If you're ready, I suggest we get down to business."

"And that business is...?"

Her brows drew together. "You asked for my help." He fixed her with a stare curiously devoid of expression and a momentary doubt seized her. "The job you came here to do? Harley called and said to get to your hotel right away. Or—or did he make a mistake?"

"What, precisely, did Harley tell you?"

"He said you wanted my advice on your current project." Madison concealed her uncertainty behind a bright smile. "I think bringing in a backup consultant is very wise of you, Harry. I'm happy to help in any way I can."

"That's very generous of you."

His voice held a quality she couldn't quite identify. Not quite sarcasm. Irony? She sighed. "Let me guess. Harley got it all wrong. I wondered why he'd have called me about it instead of Rosy."

"I suggest we go to your office where we can discuss this in a business setting."

Something was definitely wrong. Why would they need to go to *her* office to discuss *his* latest job? Nervousness gripped her and she fell back on a formality that came all too naturally. "Excellent suggestion. Are you ready?"

"Let me get my briefcase and jacket." He hesitated. "Or should we discuss yesterday first?"

Oh, dear. She lifted her chin and met his look dead-on. "I don't believe yesterday's worth discussing."

He raised an eyebrow. "Funny. I could have sworn there were several matters we should clear up."

"I can't recall any." Defiance edged her voice, betraying her inner turbulence, but she didn't care. "Nope. Not a single thing."

"Oh, no? I won't bother mentioning the most obvious one, like our kissing in the middle of a rainstorm—"

"How gracious of you," she interrupted dryly. "I appreciate your restraint."

A dangerous expression gleamed in his eyes, part aggressive demand and something more explosive, something charged with acute sexual tension. "But I'd hoped you'd at least talk to me about your parents and what happened with them."

Madison folded her arms across her chest, afraid she looked every bit as defensive as she felt. "They divorced. End of story."

"It isn't the end of the story or you wouldn't get so upset every time the subject comes up."

She decided against subtlety. She doubted it would work with someone like Harry, anyway. "Allow me to rephrase. It's the end of the story as far as you're concerned."

"For now."

He certainly knew how to set off her temper. "No! Not for now. This isn't a subject available for discussion, Harry. Not yesterday. Not today. Not ever."

"I assume that also goes for discussing your problems with commitment?"

She'd told him far too much yesterday, given him too

many liberties. And now he wanted to take advantage
of her mistake. Well, she wouldn't let him. He may be
interested in a relationship, but she wasn't. She wasn't
interested in any sort of affair. *But what if it were temporary?* an insidious voice whispered. What if she could
enjoy his company during the brief times he visited
Seattle without worrying about commitment? Just a
light, uninvolved sexual relationship that would skim the
surface and never gain access to those places she preferred to keep unseen and untouched.

He must have sensed her wavering. "Madison?"

Her name held a certain urgency, a compelling demand that almost sent her tumbling into his arms. She
teetered on the tips of her three-inch, flame-red heels. If
she didn't plan to surrender every bit of herself, she had
to get away from him. Now. She took such a hasty step
backward, her heel caught in the carpet. He was at her
side in an instant, steadying her. For a long minute their
gazes locked, their unspoken communication saying
more than words ever could. All of her fears were there
for him to read, as was his fierce determination to learn
all she fought to keep from him. It only took an instant
to recognize the stalemate and with a brief nod, Harry
released her.

"Let me grab my things and we can go," he said.

The moment he shrugged on his suit coat and picked
up his briefcase he became a different man. Madison
found it fascinating to observe. Each time they were together, Harry revealed another facet of his personality.
In the elevator he'd betrayed a gentleness she wouldn't
have believed possible if she'd seen him beforehand. His
subsequent transformation from lamb to lion had come
as an unpleasant shock. But just as she'd accustomed
herself to that, he'd morphed into the determined se-

ducer. It was the side of his personality she found the most threatening. She studied his current guise and smiled. No doubt everyone else in the world would claim this particular aspect of Harry was the most threatening—Mr. Jones, financial analyst and consummate businessman.

Sure enough, when they walked through the lobby, a half dozen people descended on them, fluttering nervously. Several were hotel management checking to make sure that Harry's accommodations met with his satisfaction. Was his suite big enough? Had they stocked it properly? Did he need additional domestic staff during his visit? Did he have any complaints? He dealt with each of them politely, yet briskly, dispensing with their services in short order.

Others, she gathered, were former business associates. To her surprise their nervousness was even more pronounced than the hotel staff. They'd heard he was in town. Anything they could do to assist him? Were recent rumors about XYZ company true? Did he have any advice/suggestions/concerns about the latest economic trends? Could he offer some clue as to his current assignment? That last question had been offered as a great joke, and might have been amusing if it hadn't been for the serious apprehension that underscored the query.

By the time the brief conversation concluded, Madison had gained the impression that Harry's presence in Seattle roused real concern among certain elements of the business community. She fought back a smile of amusement. It would seem his intimidation tactics were a great success. Certainly these men had bought into the pretense. Little did they know!

The last individual waiting to speak to Harry turned out to be an employee. "I was just on my way up." He greeted his boss. He checked his watch with an alarmed frown. "Am I late?"

Harry shook his head, quick to reassure. "Not at all, Dane. My plans have changed. Do you have the information I requested?"

"Right here, Mr. Jones." He handed over a folder. "You asked for a basic research job. If you want a more insightful report, just say the word."

"This should be fine. I'll call if I need anything else."

"Yes, sir. You have my pager number. For you, I'm available twenty-four seven."

"Thank you. I appreciate your diligence. You can take the rest of the day off."

Dane appeared stunned. "You sure?"

"Positive."

"Yes, sir. Thank you, sir!"

As soon as Dane had left, Harry glanced at an openly grinning Madison. "What's so funny?"

She tucked her hand into the crook of his arm, relieved to have them on a more comfortable footing. It reminded her of their hours together in the elevator. "I have to give you credit, Mr. Jones. You've managed to bamboozle the whole lot of them. You really do have this intimidation thing down to a science."

He lifted an eyebrow. "But I don't fool you, do I?"

"Not in the least," she confirmed cheerfully. "I'm on to your tricks."

"What if they're not tricks? What if all those people have a real reason to fear me?"

She chuckled. "Don't even try that one on me. I know you too well."

"And you're not the least intimidated?"

"Not even a little." At least, not in regards to his business dealings.

"Interesting."

It was her turn to look at him curiously. "What's interesting about it?"

"You're a novelty, Madison."

"Oh, please. I can't be the first person to realize your roar is worse than your bite."

"I thought it was bark."

"Dogs bark. Lions roar."

"So I'm a lion, just not a very intimidating one."

She gave his arm a sympathetic pat. "Don't let it upset you. I'm sure you intimidate those who aren't as shrewd a judge of character as I am." A sudden thought occurred to her. "Is that why you want my assistance with your current job? To serve as an impartial observer?"

"Not quite."

"Then it must be because I'm beautiful, brilliant and an expert when it comes to financial matters," she teased.

"True, every word. But, I'm afraid that's not it, either."

"I'm crushed."

"Wait until we get to your office. I'll answer all your questions there."

That brought her up short. It suddenly occurred to her that his business might involve her more personally than she'd first suspected. There was only one way to find out. "This has something to do with me, doesn't it?" she asked with unabashed directness.

"Let's just say that I'm a man who believes in covering all the bases and right now, you're one of the bases."

She accepted his statement with an outwardly equable nod. "I'll have to remember that."

''Wise decision.'' He stopped her before she could exit the hotel, catching hold of her elbow and turning her into his body. ''There's something else you might want to remember, as well.''

Harry could actually feel her withdrawal, her posture switching from relaxed to bristly, just as it had in his suite. He didn't care for the change. ''And what's that?'' she asked.

''You can trust me not to hurt you. You can trust me to have your best interests at heart. And you can trust me to protect you and keep you safe.'' He smiled. ''Having a scary roar can come in handy, particularly when it's backed with sharp teeth.''

Confusion softened her features, revealing a vulnerability he'd have done anything to ease. ''I don't need anyone to protect me.''

''It wasn't a multiple choice offer.''

She refused to relent. ''I suggest we keep our relationship on a business footing.''

''I'm going to do my best to change your mind.''

''You know, I'm beginning to think we're nothing alike, after all,'' she complained. ''I thought you were a reasonable man.''

''I am.''

''Reasonable—so long as I see things your way?''

He buried a smile. ''See? Perfectly reasonable.''

Aside from slanting him a look that combined exasperation with amusement, Madison didn't reply. She simply sashayed across the lobby in her eye-catching heels and bottom-hugging red skirt, completely oblivious to the attention she garnered. Harry watched in admiration. The woman never ceased to amaze him.

It didn't take them long to reach her office at the north end of the city. He was curious to see the place, won-

dering what sort of setup the Sunflowers had felt necessary for their financial advisor and family troubleshooter. The building was a small house that had
originally been a turn-of-the-century residence before the
city had overrun its boundaries. It rested in the shadow
of Queen Anne's Hill, tucked between a jumble of mod-
ern stucco office buildings and older homes that had so
far escaped conversion.

The leaded beveled-glass windows fronting the street
were originals, as was the etched-panel door. Inside, the
parlor served as a reception area and the formal dining
room across from it was an office outfitted with the latest
electronic equipment. A huge glass-and-chrome desk oc-
cupied the center of the room, at distinct odds with the
traditional surroundings. The purple-haired teenager sitting behind the desk was even more out of sync.

She eyed him through an inch-thick layer of mascara,
her expression one of deep distrust. "Don't judge by
appearances, pops," she said before he could utter a single word.

"Rosy?" He hazarded a guess.

"Like who else would it be?" Headphones hung
around her neck and she shoved them on top of her
spiked hair, adjusting the microphone so it hovered directly in front of her glossy red mouth. She stabbed an
extension on the phone with a two-inch artificial nail.
"You got Rosy. What's your problem? And it better be
good."

"She takes a little getting used to," Madison murmured.

"You think?"

"She's very good at keeping people in line."

"Now that I believe." He glanced around. "Maybe
we should talk in your office."

"It's in the back."

Rosy looked up from the note she'd been scribbling. "Sunny's on her way in. Something about yesterday's escapade. That was her word, by the way. Escapade."

Madison choked.

Black-tipped nails flicked through a stack of neon-green messages. "Harley's called four times. He wants you to know that the emergency is now a Beemer. He also complained that he hasn't been able to reach you for the past twenty-four hours." The small hoop earring decorating the end of Rosy's eyebrow punctuated her questioning glance. "What did you do? Turn off your cell?"

"It drowned."

"That must have been one hell of a picnic."

"Anything else?" Harry interrupted.

She turned to look at him, a blue-eyed glare finding its way through all the mascara. "Funny. I could have sworn I was talkin' to Madison."

Smart-mouthed brat. "Wrong. Your employer is going to her office while you and I enjoy a brief conversation. Then I'll be joining her and you're going to hold all her calls. Now is there anything else you need to tell her before that happens?"

Madison started to intercede. One glimpse of his expression and she spun on her heel and stalked down the hallway. Something about the irritable swing of her hips warned that he'd be hearing about his presumptuousness.

Rosy shook her head in admiration. "You're one tough hombre. I'll give you that."

"I've also got the muscle to back up my mouth. How about you?"

"Hell, no," she scoffed. "It's all talk."

A swift grin slashed across his face. "At least you're

honest.'' His smile faded. ''Now explain to me why Harley told Madison we'd be working together. Because I'm going to take him apart piece by piece if I don't like the answer.''

Rosy's eyes narrowed to two black smears. ''Why should that upset you? It's the truth, isn't it?''

''It's a possibility. I hadn't decided whether to accept the job. I'm here for other reasons, if you'll recall. You may also recall that *if* I decided to accept the assignment, I'd be the one explaining it to Madison.''

Rosy shrugged. ''Go explain. No one's stopping you.''

He fought for control. What was it about these Sunflowers? He'd never met so many people with so little regard for self-preservation. ''Then the idea was actually yours?''

She snorted. ''I'm not that stupid. This was Harley's brilliant notion.'' She had the nerve to laugh. ''I think he got it from one of your rules. Something about working together and having Important Discussions. Sound familiar, Jones?''

Harry gritted his teeth, holding on to his temper by a thread. ''Tell Harley I want to speak to him. In fact, tell your entire family I want to see them. For now, I'm going to have one of those Important Discussions with Madison. Do *not* let anyone interrupt us. Understood?''

''I think I can handle it.''

''Make very sure you do.''

Harry left Rosy's office, turning in the same direction Madison had gone. There were two doors at the end of the hallway, one leading to a small, efficient kitchen, another into what must have once been a living room but now served as Madison's office. He entered the room and closed the door behind him, looking around with pleasure.

With the exception of Rosy's desk, the entire house had been decorated in golden oaks and warm antique white walls. This room was no exception. But there was more, a definite essence of Madison's presence that permeated the office, exuding a feminine charm captured within an efficient business-like setting. The couch and chairs were upholstered in a sunny yellow and bowls of fresh cut flowers accented the simple, natural wood furnishings. The total effect came across as cheerful, welcoming and—he couldn't help smiling—practical.

Madison sat behind her desk and regarded him with a stoic expression. The look didn't surprise him. She was a smart woman. The fact that she hadn't figured out certain aspects of his presence long before this spoke more to her trusting nature and a certain amount of personal distraction than to a lack of intelligence or business acumen.

"Your family doesn't seem to understand the concept of intimidation," he offered as a conversational gambit.

She inclined her head. "That must be very frustrating for you."

"I'll survive." Though Harley's life expectancy remained in question.

"What did you need to talk to Rosy about?"

"I asked her why Harley told you to come to my hotel room to discuss our mutual business interests."

"*Our* business interests." She took a moment to absorb that and he waited for the inevitable questions. The first one she chose to ask, though, took him by surprise. "Does it matter who told me?"

"Yes. Your family knew I'd planned to initiate the discussion with you in my own good time and in my own way."

She nodded as though he'd confirmed her suspicions. "Just out of curiosity... When would that have been? Before you'd seduced me or after?"

CHAPTER SEVEN

*Principle 7: Trust, Honesty,
and the Honorable Way, Or...
What to tell your partner about your past!*

"OH, IT definitely would have been after I seduced
you," Harry assured her. "To be honest, your seduction
topped my list of priorities. My business interests with
you come dead last."

Madison shoved back her chair and stood. "This isn't
a joke."

"I'm glad you agree."

She turned and crossed to the French doors behind her
desk. They opened onto a walled garden overrun with
flowers. "Why are you here, Harry? And I'd appreciate
the truth this time."

"That isn't what you want to know." He came up
behind her and she stiffened, her tension communicating
itself in the rigid set of her shoulders and the ramrod
alignment of her spine. "Ask your real question."

"The men at the hotel were speculating about your
current project...who, what, where." She turned just
enough to risk a glance in his direction. He could see
the devastation he'd caused and he swore beneath his
breath. There ought to be an iron-clad rule about mixing
business with pleasure—one he stuck to. Next time,
there would be. "I'm your project, aren't I?" she asked.

In more ways than she could ever guess. "Yes."

"Which means I'm Dane's research assignment. I'm also the favor Bartholomew asked of you." The faintest tremor of her chin betrayed her and she returned to studying the garden. "You mentioned the favor when we were trapped on the elevator. You're supposed to take a look at my operation and see whether or not I'm doing an adequate job for my family, aren't you?"

Their discussion wasn't proceeding the way he'd planned. His business matters rarely went this drastically askew, which made it all the more annoying that it would happen now, when the stakes were so high and the ultimate objective so vital. He shook his head in exasperation. But then, very little about this assignment had anything to do with business. Perhaps that explained why fate seemed determined to screw him over.

"I told my father I'd consider checking out your operation," he admitted. "But I wanted to get a feel for you and how you ran things before I determined whether it was worthwhile interfering."

"Because we're such small potatoes?"

He smiled. "Very small. But that's not why I hesitated."

"Then why?"

The tremor in her chin had invaded her voice. He wanted to gather her close, to hold her while he explained. She deserved whatever reassurances he could offer, as well as an apology for allowing matters to get so far out of hand. He started to reach out, but an untouchable remoteness encompassed her, warning she wouldn't appreciate or accept his attempt to comfort. His arms dropped to his sides. *Work the main problem, Jones.* If he kept the personal aspects out of it for now, he might be able to see this thing through with minimal damage.

"I hesitated taking on this job because it isn't strictly business," he told her.

Madison took a moment to absorb his explanation before rejecting it with a single shake of her head. "Piffle."

Tiny ringlets had escaped the intricate knot she'd anchored at the nape of her neck, the wayward curls providing a striking counterpoint to her rigid control. In fact, she sent out a barrage of mixed messages today.

She wore a severely cut suit, perfect for the office if it weren't for the fact that it was street-corner red. Flaming stiletto heels decorated her feet, the dainty scraps of leather more appropriate for a hot night on the town than a day spent hiding beneath a desk. Her slicked-back hair was the severest style she'd worn to date, yet it exposed the most vulnerable and appealing nape he'd ever seen. And though her makeup was elegantly applied, her mouth had been lushly outlined in a wicked kiss-me-*now* shade that echoed the color of her suit.

It all added up to a woman who hadn't quite decided whether today would be spent focused on business or on the man with whom she was conducting that business. It gave him the first shred of hope he'd experienced since arriving at her office.

"You said you were hesitant about taking on this job." She splayed her hand across a small beveled windowpane set in the door, the gesture one of unconscious appeal. It was a dead giveaway. It didn't take any effort on his part to realize she was reaching toward the sanctuary offered by the garden, a world of natural beauty and serenity containing none of the current turmoil swirling through her office. "What have you decided? Are you going to look us over or not?"

"Now that's an interesting question." The curls beck-

oned him, begging to be twined around his fingers. He
ignored the insidious temptation. "To be honest, I have
to weigh my options."

"And what options are those?"

He reached around her and ran his index finger over
the top of hers. "First consideration... How will business affect our relationship?"

She stilled at the tantalizing touch. "It won't," she
whispered. "Because we don't have a relationship."

"Liar." He stroked her middle finger. "Second consideration... If I take a look at your operation, will you
resent my interference?"

This time she shivered. "Yes. But only because it's
not necessary."

He caressed her ring finger. "Third consideration...
And this one isn't a question, but a statement of fact. If
I don't take a look, you'll always wonder."

Madison snatched her hand from beneath his and
turned, her eyes dilating when she discovered how close
he stood. "What will I wonder?"

"Whether you would have won."

"This isn't a game, Harry." Passion infused her
voice, underscoring how seriously she took their discussion. "This is my life."

"We're the same, you and I." He said it more as a
warning than an observation. "You've been pointing
that out ever since we first met. I know how you'll react
if I take a walk. You'll wonder if I would have found a
way to improve your family's financial situation. You'll
start questioning your decisions, playing guessing games
with yourself that you can't win, speculating whether or
not I'd have made a different choice from the one you
made, until the doubt eats you alive."

"Not a chance," she insisted. "I'm good at my job. In fact, I'm better than good."

"Then you don't have anything to worry about, do you?"

Her eyes went dark with pain. "Oh, no?"

He released his breath in a long sigh. Hell. She knew. "Madison—"

"Bartholomew wouldn't have asked you to step in unless someone from the family had requested it."

He'd hoped she wouldn't make that connection. Now that she had, he'd deal with it head-on. "Sunny asked him." His response impacted like a blow, even though it could only have confirmed what she'd suspected. "I'm sorry, sweetheart. I didn't plan to tell you like this."

"How were you going to do it?" The question escaped through stiff, white lips. In fact, everything about her had gone pale, at striking opposition to the darkness of her hair and eyes and the profusion of color at her back. "Were you going to find a way to make it seem like this was all my idea? Have me ask for your services, one financial advisor to another?"

"Something like that. Unfortunately, Harley decided to interfere."

Anger eclipsed the hurt. "Did you really think I wouldn't have seen through the deception?" she demanded. "That I wouldn't have gotten suspicious at some point?"

"The truth would have come out eventually. I would have made sure it did. But I hoped to limit the impact, as well as the damage." He gave in to temptation and smoothed a curl from her brow. "Instead, I've managed to make it worse. And I'm sorry about that."

She sidestepped his touch. "You should have told me what you were up to from the beginning."

"When? On the elevator while you were fighting claustrophobia?" He struggled to conceal his exasperation. "Should I have said, 'Oh, by the way, your family has asked me to check out what sort of job you're doing'?"

"Yes!" Another barrage of curls escaped her control, an outward expression of her inner turmoil. They rioted around her face in fiery disorder, spitfire ringlets that voiced her indignation more vehemently than mere words. "At least then it would have been out in the open and we could have dealt with the situation honestly."

"I wasn't certain whether or not I'd take the job. I didn't see any point in saying anything until I'd made that decision."

"But you have now." She didn't phrase it as a question.

"Yes." Dammit all! "I'm sorry, Madison. I promised not to hurt you and I've managed to do just that."

"You also promised to have my best interests at heart." Her kissable mouth compressed into an unkissable line. "I'd say you failed on all accounts."

"You're wrong about that. You can't see it now because you're too upset. But I promise, having me look over the family business will clear the air between us. It'll put business to one side and allow us to concentrate on personal issues."

She cut him off with a sweep of her hand. "There are no personal issues! Not anymore. You deceived me and I don't take that well. Not well at all. I need to trust the people in my life, especially when it comes to business."

"You still don't get it." He closed the distance between them. "Having me work with you has nothing to do with business."

She regarded him impatiently, but at least she didn't

back away. "What are you talking about?" she demanded.

"Oh, come on. You have to know your grandmother better than that. It's not like she's been particularly subtle about it." When Madison continued to stare blankly, he clarified. "Sunny doesn't want me looking over the family finances because she thinks you're doing a bad job. She's matchmaking."

Madison gave a heartbreaking little laugh. "You're wrong. Her doubts about my ability are precisely what this is about."

"No—"

"You don't understand, Harry," she interrupted. "You don't have all the facts."

"Then tell me. What am I missing?"

She drew a ragged breath and met his gaze, her expression resolute. "I'm an Adams, the daughter of Wilson Adams. That's why they asked you to check up on me. They want to make sure that I wasn't corrupted by my father, that I'm not following in his footsteps."

Her certainty stopped him cold. "Explain."

"I'm sorry they put you in the middle." She averted her gaze, visibly withdrawing, her emotions concealed behind a dispassionate calm. Even her curls had stilled their vivacious dance. "Never mind. I'll handle it from here."

The hell she would. "I'm not going anywhere, Madison. Not until you tell me what this is about."

"You want the sordid details?"

"Why do I have the feeling I'm supposed to take the high road and say no?" he muttered.

Wry humor flickered through her gaze, the first hint of amusement he'd seen since they'd arrived at her office. "Wishful thinking on my part, I guess."

He considered doing as she asked, shaking his head when he realized he couldn't. "I'm sorry, sweetheart. I can't let it go. Tell me how your father is involved in all this."

She shrugged. "Okay. Assuming Sunny and Bartholomew really do get married, you'd have heard the story eventually." She turned toward the French doors and thrust them open. "Let's go outside. We can talk there."

He followed, pausing at the edge of the grass. The morning light flooded the yard, providing a warm welcome. Cedar chip walkways bordered in begonias criss-crossed the small yard and a set of wooden benches placed beside a massive rhododendron offered a pretty resting spot at the far back of the property. Haphazard flowerbeds spilled onto the neatly trimmed grass, teeming with every possible variety of flower and herb.

Someone had put a lot of time and effort into the place and Harry suspected he knew who. The garden "felt" like Madison, the abundance of color suited to her vivid appearance. "Nice. Is this where you play?"

She nodded, confirming his guess. "I've found gardening a terrific stress reliever. You should have seen it a few years ago. It was a mess." She looked around with satisfaction. "It's been quite a learning experience. I'd barely even picked a flower before giving this a try. It was sort of trial and error for a while there."

True, the garden hadn't been designed by a professional landscaper. Flowers overran everything in an impractical, enthusiastic jumble as though this was the one place in her life she could safely release all controls and act with spontaneous abandon. But Harry found the overall effect appealing. It was also apparent that the garden had been cared for by a loving hand, free of weeds and pests, and well fertilized. Dozens of competing scents perfumed the air, anchored by the rich, earthy odor of freshly tilled soil, the combination melding into an appealing whole. After a few minutes in her garden Madison visibly relaxed and a healthy flush returned to her cheekbones.

She took her time, wandering to the fence marking the end of her property. Every few steps she bent to pull a weed or pinch off a faded bloom. "I think I mentioned that my father was an accountant," she finally said.

"You told me you'd inherited your practical nature from him."

"Yes. Dad was always…practical." She stooped beside an aggressive clump of mint even though it caused the points of her stiletto heels to sink into the dew-laden grass. Harry had the distinct impression she did it to avoid his gaze. The fact that it was so out of character riveted his attention. "Dad was also one of the most amoral men I've ever known. He was a thief and a liar."

Harry grimaced. Hell. He hadn't seen that one coming. "I gather that's not just idle speculation?"

"No. In the years he was married to my mother, he systematically stripped the Sunflowers of most of their assets."

Harry crouched beside Madison while he considered her claim. Grasping her elbow so she wouldn't lose her balance, he removed first one of her shoes, then the other.

She frowned at him in exasperation. "What are you doing?"

"Keeping you from ruining your shoes."

"What possible difference does it make if they get wrecked?"

He cradled the scraps of leather in his hands and regarded them with a smile. "This may come as news to you, but men fantasize about shoes like this."

"Want to try them on?" she asked dryly.

His smile grew. "No, sweetheart. Aside from the fact that I couldn't fit much more than my big toe in them, they suit you far better. Actually, they'd suit you best if you wore these and as little else as possible." He fired his next question at her before she had time to do more than stare at him in stunned disbelief. "Did Sunny tell you Wilson had stolen the Sunflowers's money?"

She looked like she preferred to discuss the shoes some more—anything to avoid their previous conversation—but finally shook her head. "No. Sunny never said a word."

"Then who?"

She stood and walked barefoot to the next flowerbed, throwing her reply over her shoulder almost as an afterthought. "Dad told me."

"Wait a minute." Harry caught up with her and turned her around. Without her heels she appeared small and fragile and painfully defenseless. There was also a look of such bleakness in her eyes that if their conversation hadn't been so vital, he'd have gathered her in his arms and talked about anything and everything other than their current topic. But instinct warned that he should get to the bottom of this, that it was at the core of all that stood between them. "Let me get this straight. Your father admitted he stole from your own mother?"

For the first time since he'd met her, she refused to meet his gaze, staring at a point somewhere over his right shoulder. "He was quite up front about it. Proud, even."

"I don't get it. Why would he have confessed to you?"

"Confessed?" Her quiet laugh floated on the warm air, the underlying anguish painful to hear. She wrapped her arms around herself. "It wasn't a confession, Harry. He was bragging. He wanted me to admire his cleverness."

"That son of a—" He bit off the rest of what he'd planned to say. Wilson Adams might be a bastard, but he was still her father. "What did your mother do? You told her what he'd said, didn't you?"

He'd asked the wrong question. Tears filled Madison's eyes, and the calm she'd fought to maintain fractured, her pain too great to contain any longer. "No, I didn't tell her."

"Why, Madison?" he demanded. "Why didn't you tell your mother?"

The first tear fell. "I couldn't find her."

He didn't hesitate. He swept her into his arms and carried her to the wooden benches beside the rhododendron. He held her without speaking for a long time, letting her cry her way through what must have been the most traumatic time of her life. When she finally lifted her head, she swiped at his suit coat with shaking fingers.

"I've made a mess of your jacket."

"Like I give a damn." He slid his hand into her hair, the silky curls wrapping around his fingers in vibrant welcome. "Do you want to tell me the rest?"

"There's not much left to explain."

He forced himself to intrude a little further. "What happened to your mother?"

"Dad divorced her. He was awarded custody of me by the courts." She'd managed to recover most of her control, but a wealth of emotion came through in those two simple statements. "That's why I couldn't find my mother. He took me as far from her as he could."

"*He* won custody? How did he manage that?"

"I told you. The Adamses consist mainly of accountants and lawyers, with a few bankers thrown in for good measure. They're very skilled at what they do. Very methodical. They make a living at corrupting all that's good and helpful about those professions. My mother never stood a chance. Dad portrayed her and the rest of her family as kooks and nutcases, a danger to my well-being. I still don't know all the specifics, just that when I walked into the courtroom it was surrounded by Sunflowers. And when I was carried out by my father, it was kicking and screaming the entire way."

"How old were you?"

"Ten."

"Where's your father now?" Maybe he shouldn't ask. He might be tempted to do something about it.

She shrugged. "Back east." Her mouth twisted. "We don't talk much anymore."

"And your mother?"

"She took off for Europe after the divorce. She shows up every once in a while."

So Madison had lost both mother and father. No wonder she was so contained. She must have learned the behavior long ago out of sheer self-preservation. "When did you return to Seattle?"

"The day I turned eighteen. I'd always planned to, even as a little girl. From the minute my father took me east, I dreamed of finding a way back home. I used to secretly call myself Dorothy after *The Wizard of Oz*. Whenever things got really bad I'd tap my shoes together and beg to be sent home." Her smile held a wistful quality. "It never worked, but I kept trying anyway. When I finally came of age, I didn't have to tap my shoes. I simply pointed them west, started walking, and didn't stop until I found Sunny.''

"What happened then?"

"I went to college and learned everything I could about how to fix all the damage my father had caused. And since graduating I've spent the last four years putting right all of his wrongs.'' Madison escaped Harry's arms. Snatching her shoes from his hands, she slipped them on her feet. Armored with the extra few inches they provided, she faced him with a hint of her old defiance. "You may not believe this, but I'm very good at my job. The Sunflowers were almost bankrupt when I arrived here. In the few short years I've had control of their assets, I've restored everything my father destroyed, and then some. I even bought back the family home.''

"I don't doubt it.'' He stood, as well. "But the one thing nobody seems to have bothered to explain to you is that Wilson's actions weren't your fault. You don't have to keep paying for them.''

"I'm not paying, I'm protecting,'' she corrected. "There's a big difference. So long as I'm in control, my family's safe from my father and every other con artist who's tempted to take advantage of them.''

He steered her back to the original discussion. "And you think that because your father embezzled from the Sunflowers, they've asked me to step in and check up on you? Make sure you aren't your father's daughter?''

"What other reason could there be?'' Tears welled into her eyes again and she visibly fought them back. This time she succeeded, her determination to hold her emotions at bay painful to witness. "Not that I blame them. It's a sensible precaution.''

He proceeded with care. "Yes, it is. And yes, it would

be, if we were dealing with sensible people. But since we're not, I think you need to consider the possibility that there's another reason for their request.''

''You mean your matchmaking theory.''

''Yes.''

She shook her head and her hands balled into fists, warning that her control was more fragile than it appeared. ''It's ridiculous to think Sunny's request is motivated by a desire to set us up.''

''It's ridiculous to think that's not her reason,'' he argued. ''She has no business acumen, from what you've said. It isn't logical to believe she'd acquire it at this late date. If you want to find out the real reason for her interference, it's simple. We'll ask her.''

''No! I won't put Sunny in such an embarrassing position.''

''Honey, Sunny doesn't know the meaning of the word 'embarrassing.' I guarantee she'd be very upset to think you'd misinterpreted her actions.'' He could tell he hadn't convinced her. ''Okay, fine. We won't mention our discussion to your grandmother. Instead, I'll take a look at your setup. And you'll cooperate.''

''Why should I?''

''Because it's what your family wants and it will put paid to your suspicions. If they continue to push us together, even after I've completed my examination, you can safely assume that's why Sunny concocted this scheme. Fair enough?''

''Is that my only choice?''

''No.'' He tugged her into his arms, pleasantly surprised when she wrapped her arms around his neck and lifted her face to his. ''You can accept what your relatives are offering without complaint or argument.''

''And what are they offering?''

He lowered his head until their mouths were a mere whisper apart. "Me."

Her lashes fluttered closed and he kissed her. She was so soft, so giving, so eager. And yet, he knew it wouldn't last. Too many secrets remained that would drive a wedge between them when they ultimately came out. But at least the first one had been dealt with and he hadn't lost her.

Time would tell how she handled the others.

"I don't know how we're going to top Dell and Harley," Daniel announced, slumping into the chair next to Rosy's desk. "They've been quite helpful. Thanks to them, Harry and Madison have spent the last week working together without a single argument."

"Oh, there have been plenty of arguments. They've just led to these long, disgusting silences." Rosy scowled, drumming her three-inch, neon-green-spackled fingernails on her desktop. "I just know they're doin' it on her desk. Try and find *that* rule in Jones's book."

Daniel squirmed in his chair. "I'm sure I don't recall anything about desks."

"Trust me, I've looked—twice—and it isn't there."

"Oh, dear."

Rosy tossed her telephone headset onto the desk in utter disgust. "You've got that right. Who'd have thought Harley and Dell could have pulled off so much as one rule, let alone two. And so successfully. Those idiots are a prime example of incompetence stumbling into disaster and falling flat onto success. Unbelievable. They really fry my a—" One glimpse of Daniel's wide-eyed stared had her changing her phrasing. "They really fry my acorns."

"What should we do?"

She gave it some thought. "I suppose it's too much to hope that we can stumble from incompetence to disaster and fall flat on success, too?"

"I'm afraid it might be."

"That's what I thought you'd say." She drummed some more. "But if we don't butt in and soon, Harry and Madison might not even need our help."

Her uncle shook his head. "I'm sorry, my dear. I don't see how we can top your cousin and aunt."

"Well, we're gonna try." She shot him a warning glare. "And we're gonna do it without you ending up in jail for being too helpful. Understand?"

"But I like helping."

"Tough. That judge told you to knock it off and you better listen to him and not that slimy lawyer."

"Mr. Bryant doesn't seem to mind it when I get into trouble."

"Of course not! He rakes in a bundle every time you do." This wasn't getting them anywhere. "How many rules do we have left to choose from?"

Daniel pried open the book and flipped through the pages. "Not many. Something about perfection and—" He broke off with a blush. "Oh, my."

"Sex," Rosy guessed, grinning in satisfaction. "Perfect. I can do sex."

"I did not hear that!"

"Sure you did. You just didn't want to." She leaned forward and patted Daniel's hand. "Don't worry. I'll take care of everything. You won't have to lift a finger and I'll even give you partial credit."

"Please, Rosy. I'd really rather you didn't involve me at all. Not if it's about—"

"Relax. This is gonna be lots better than jail. You'll

see.'' She glanced down the hallway toward Madison's office with a sly smile. ''It'll sure as hell be better than a desk, which I'm hopin' those two will find out real soon.''

CHAPTER EIGHT

Principle 8: Perfection doesn't exist.
So, what's really important to you?

"STOP being so stubborn, Madison."

"Stubborn?" She glared at Harry. "You have a lot of nerve calling me stubborn. We went over Harley's portfolio three days ago. Why are we doing it again?"

"I still have some questions about his IRA."

"It's a standard retirement account, Harry. There's nothing the least questionable about it." She planted her hands on her hips and regarded him with acute suspicion. "If I didn't know better, I'd swear you were stalling."

"Explain."

He folded his arms across his chest and fixed her with his best I'm-the-terror-of-the-business-world-and-you'd-better-start-trembling look. He also liked to chop up his words into hard demanding nuggets whenever he hoped to rattle her. On the whole it was quite unnerving. Perhaps it had something to do with his impressive height or the even more impressive shape stretching his suit to the limits. Not that any of that actually succeeded at unnerving her. Good heavens, no. She knew better than to allow such ridiculous tactics to work. Men like Harry Jones needed someone capable of standing up to them. And she was the perfect woman for the job.

She shook Harley's file under his nose. "You've gone

over every portfolio, account, and record that I have in this office. Now you want to start at the beginning and do it all over again?" She slapped the file onto her desk. "There can only be one explanation."

"Which is?"

"You're stalling."

"Why would I do that?"

"Gee, I don't know, Harry." Exasperation edged her voice along with a healthy dose of sarcasm. "I don't suppose it has anything to do with keeping me from interfering with Sunny and Bartholomew's engagement?"

He lifted a single eyebrow, another of his cute little gestures. Actually, she found it irritatingly endearing. More often than not it expressed an element of wry humor. And more often than not she ended up dissolving into laughter. Maybe that's why he did it. He seemed to like her laugh, a tender light filling his hazel eyes. She frowned. When had they developed such an intimate understanding of each other? She suspected it originated the day he'd held her in his arms while she'd told him about her childhood.

"I'm shocked. You weren't planning on interfering with your grandmother's engagement, were you?" he asked.

"Of course not." At his continued silence, she shrugged, compelled to honesty. "At least, not much. I just want to make sure they're not rushing into anything."

"That's what I thought." He picked up the folder she'd discarded. "Shall we take another look at your cousin's investments?"

"Not a chance. Not when there isn't any point. I've

done an incredible job these past four years. Admit it, Harry.''

"You've done an incredible job.''

"Then we're through?''

The tender light she'd noticed earlier warmed into something more passionate. "Not by a long shot. There's still a lot left for us to accomplish.''

"None of which has anything to do with Sunflower business, I gather.''

A knock at the door saved him from having to reply and Rosy trotted into the office. "Hey, Jones. Some guy phoned who claims he's a former client. He says it's urgent and call him back right away. You gonna do what he says or should I tell him to go to hell for you?''

"Does he have a name?''

"Yeah. Bradford.''

Her expression turned sly and Madison winced, wondering if Harry was familiar with that particular look or whether she should give him a heads up. Oh, why bother? It would be a lot more fun to watch him deal with whatever scheme her devious cousin had in mind.

"I don't suppose he's related to the computer game people?'' Rosy asked.

"He's not related to them, no.'' Harry paused a beat. "He *is* the computer game people.''

Rosy grinned. "I was hoping you'd say that.'' She crossed the room and rattled a piece of paper in his face. "Here. This is for you.''

Harry regarded it warily. "What is it?''

"A list. When you go take care of his emergency, make him give you the games I wrote down. They're not out yet, and I can't wait any longer for them.''

"Not a chance.''

She narrowed her eyes, long mascara spears jutted

fiercely in his direction. "So you're sayin' you're a big shot, just not that big."

Taking advantage of Harry's distraction, Madison twitched Harley's file from between his fingers and buried it beneath a stack of papers on her desk. "I'm disappointed," she baited in an undertone. "Here I thought you could do anything."

"Hell." He snatched the paper from Rosy's hand and glared at her. "If I didn't owe you—" he muttered.

"Yeah, yeah." She swaggered across the room, her microscopic skirt swishing against the tops of her thighs. Turning at the door, she puckered her purple-coated lips and blew him a kiss. "Save the huffing and puffing for someone whose house blows down easy, Jones. Big bad wolves don't scare me."

"How about lions?" he shot back. "Do they make you nervous? Because I have it on good authority that I have an excellent roar."

Her only response was a gurgling laugh better suited to a schoolgirl than the smart-mouthed hard-case she preferred to impersonate.

Madison waited until the door closed before confronting Harry. "Okay, spill it. What do you owe her and why?"

Instantly, his business mask slammed into place. "It's a personal matter."

"What sort of—"

"I have a suggestion," he interrupted smoothly. "Why don't you come with me when I call on Bradford?"

She wasn't about to let him get away with that one. "Are you asking in order to change the subject?"

"The subject has been changed. You just haven't realized it yet." The lion had definitely taken over, his roar loud and clear. "I'm asking you to come along for another reason altogether."

Madison reached a decision. She'd let her questions about Rosy go for now. She could always bring it up when she required a quick change of topics herself. Besides, this sounded far more interesting than another day spent analyzing spreadsheets and financial plans. "All right, I'll come. Although I'd like you to explain why you've suddenly decided I should."

"This has been a good week. We've had a few squabbles, sure. But you have to admit there's something happening between us."

She didn't bother denying it. They couldn't look at each other without wanting to touch. And they couldn't touch each other without needing to kiss. Soon the kisses would lead other places, places she wasn't certain she could resist. "What does our relationship have to do with Bradford?"

An odd tension filled him, stealing some of the grace from his movements. "I want you to know who I am. I want you to see the whole man, not just various aspects."

It took her a minute to realize what he was saying. "Oh, Harry," she murmured in dismay. "Are you worried that my opinion will alter once I see you on the job? That my feelings for you might change?"

His demeanor turned even more intense. "Something like that."

"But I've seen that side of you. We've spent the last week working together."

"Not quite. We've spent the last week playing at work."

"How can you say that?" she demanded indignantly. "You call what you've put me through playing?"

He flashed a quick smile. "I've been having fun. Haven't you?"

"Not really." Though spending time with him had been wonderful. "Okay, maybe a little."

"I can show you the difference between work and play." He held out his hand. "All you have to do is come with me."

It was unquestionably a challenge. She took his proffered hand, unable to resist lacing her fingers through his. "You're on."

"Let me call Bradford and tell him we're on our way."

"And then I'll see the real Harry Jones?"

He didn't laugh as she'd intended. "You'll see a big part of him."

"A big part, huh?" She couldn't resist teasing him a little more. "You say that like you have a small part. If so, you've kept it well hidden."

"Anytime you want to see it, feel free to ask."

She shook her head. "You disappoint me, Harry. I thought everything about you would be larger than life."

"Can it, Adams, or I'll give you a preview right here and now and you can offer your professional opinion on the matter."

"There's only one problem with that," she informed him seriously.

"What?"

"I can't promise it would be a professional opinion. But it definitely would be the opinion of an interested party." She snatched her hand from his and sauntered to the door in a perfect imitation of Rosy. Once there, she paused long enough to shoot him a wicked grin. "A *very* interested party."

*   *   *

"Madison, I'd like you to meet Kent Bradford, President and CEO of Bradford Software."

Madison offered her hand, hoping her astonishment wasn't too apparent. The kid Harry introduced didn't look old enough to have climbed out of a sandbox by himself, let alone run a major software company. "A pleasure to meet you, Mr. Bradford."

"Call me Kent." A quick, infectious grin slid across his face. "And I'm twenty-two."

She grimaced. "Was I that obvious?"

"Nah. You were real subtle. Hardly even blinked. The only one who's never reacted was this guy." He balled up a fist and actually had the nerve to sock Harry's arm. Not that it made any impression. Instead, Kent winced, shaking his bruised fingers. "Don't think anything rattles him."

"So what's the problem, Bradford?" Clearly, Harry didn't intend to waste his breath on pleasantries. "I thought we had you all straightened out."

In an instant the joking boy turned into a grim-faced man. "I thought so, too. But over the past three months something's gone wrong. Major league wrong."

"What?"

"I'm not sure. That's why I called you."

"Give me the short version."

Kent shrugged. "Okay. I'm losing money. Lots of it. And I don't know how or why or where it's going."

"That's not my department. My job is to tell you what to do with your money once you get it, remember? Not where to find it when it goes missing."

"I know, I know. But there's no one else I can trust."

"Hire an auditor."

"I did. They couldn't find anything."

"Was it one of the firms I recommended?"

"No," Kent admitted. "They weren't available right away. I went with a smaller, local outfit, instead."

"Then I suggest you quit wasting my time and call in the big guns. If they can't find anything, I'll come back and take another look."

Madison winced. If this was the side Harry wanted to show her, she could live without it. "We're here now," she cut in. "What would it hurt to spend a day poking around?"

Kent turned to her, his relief palpable. "Thanks, I'd really appreciate anything you can do. You see, my company took off a bit ahead of schedule and I wasn't ready for it. That's when I first called in Harry. He told me how to handle the explosion before someone decided to take advantage of my stupidity."

Harry shifted his stance and that was all it took. Kent fell silent. Score one for the lion, Madison thought. "Since it would seem we're staying—courtesy of Ms. Adams's compassionate nature, I might add—I suggest we get down to business. Tell me specifically what changes you've made in the last three months that might correspond with the time frame we're talking about with the missing money."

"For starters I've divided the company like you recommended and hired people to head each division from that list you gave me," Kent began. "We've subcontracted the manufacturing. The game revenue is being divvied up the way you advised and we're getting ready to go public with our stock. Just recently, I hired a bunch of pencil pushers to keep the records straight, money guys to make sure the funds go where they're supposed to, and lawyers to take care of all the necessary lawyering."

"Sounds like you're on the right track."

"Yeah, you've turned me into a real businessman." Kent scowled. "And I *will* get even for that."

Harry managed a brief smile. "Okay, Bradford. You've got me for one day. Just make sure you're extra nice to Madison since she's the one who's convinced me to stay."

Kent nodded. "Anything you want, Harry, it's yours." Then he winked at Madison. "You're a sweetheart. I promise I'll find a way to make it up to you."

She immediately thought of Rosy's request. "I may have the perfect means for you to do that. Remind me before we leave."

Once again Harry shifted his stance and once more he gained instant attention. "Time's wasting, so I suggest we play this low key," he advised. "First, I'll need a secretary—someone smart enough to keep his or her mouth shut about why we're here. I'll also need a computer terminal and any passwords necessary to access your various departments and systems."

"Five minutes and you'll have that, along with some of the best coffee your taste buds have ever encountered," Kent promised.

The next several hours proved a revelation for Madison. It didn't take more than fifteen minutes of laboring alongside Harry to realize just what he'd meant when he'd claimed to be "playing" at work this past week. She'd never seen anyone with such focus and drive. One by one, he progressed through the various departments, showing her how to analyze the information before moving on. She'd expected him to call in the heads of each division. When he didn't, she questioned him about it.

"If money's disappearing, someone's responsible," he explained. "If I start calling people in, the guilty party is going to get wind of the investigation and take off. If I can surprise him, we have a chance of recovering some of the money. I'm hoping the fact that he survived a preliminary audit may have made him cocky. If we're really lucky, it'll also have made him careless.''

Late that afternoon, Kent showed up again. ''Anything?'' he asked with a hint of desperation.

Harry shook his head. ''I have to tell you, Bradford, nothing's jumping out at me. I'm not a professional auditor, but on the surface everything looks clean. Whoever's doing this has covered his tracks well. I have accounts receivable and payable left to go through and that's about it.''

Kent appeared utterly dejected. ''That's Linc's department. I don't expect you'll find anything there.''

Madison's head jerked up. ''Linc?''

Kent managed a hint of his former joviality. ''Linc Smith. He's even more of a kid than I am. Real smart, despite being a snot-nosed brat. Never saw a number he couldn't crunch.''

Madison fought to draw breath. No. Please, no. ''And this Linc... He writes all the checks?''

''Most of them, I guess. At least, that's what I hired him to do. Why?''

She glanced toward Harry. ''I know you don't want to involve any of the department heads, but I think we should pay Linc a visit.''

He didn't even hesitate. ''Fine. Let's go.''

Kent reached for the phone on Harry's desk. ''I'll give him a quick call and tell him we're on our way down.''

Madison took the phone out of his hands and gently returned the receiver to the cradle. ''Why don't we make it a surprise visit,'' she suggested. ''And why don't we do it *now*.''

Nodding in agreement, Kent crossed to the door. But Harry hung back. "What's wrong?" he murmured.

She kept her voice low, as well. "Could be nothing."

"But you don't think so."

She shook her head. "I'm pretty sure we'll be able to clear up Mr. Bradford's problems today. But I doubt he'll be happy with what we find."

"I'm willing to bet he knew that even before he called us in."

Madison touched Harry's arm and the biceps bunched beneath her fingers, warning of his sensitivity to her touch. It would seem she affected him as keenly as he affected her. "Harry?" He simply waited, his gaze watchful, and she forced herself to continue. "You're not going to be happy with what we find, either. In fact, you're probably going to be very angry."

"Why?"

He was biting off his words already. She peeked uneasily at Kent who stared at them with open curiosity. "I'd rather not explain until I'm certain of my facts. Just don't say I didn't warn you."

Accounting was on the lower level of the building and the three of them took the elevator without speaking. Kent had picked up on her anxiety and an unnatural strain settled on his youthful features. The door to Linc's office was closed and Harry took the lead, opening it without knocking.

Madison stepped into the office first. One glance confirmed her worst fears. "Hello, Lincoln," she greeted her younger cousin. "I was hoping I wouldn't find you here."

"Madison!" A variety of emotions swept across his face—astonishment, followed by anxiety, before a blustery panic set in. "What's going on?"

"I think you know." She fought for calm. "I see Dad's brought you into the family business."

"I'm an accountant, if that's what you mean."

She began to tremble and nothing she tried would stop it. Not balling her hands into fists, nor gritting her teeth, nor using the silly mantra that Aunt Dell intoned whenever she got lost and was on the verge of panicking. Not even having Harry at her back helped. Instead, it only seemed to make it worse. "Accounting isn't the family business and you know it. At least, it's not the real one."

"And what is the family business?" Kent bit out.

Hot color blazed in Madison's cheeks and she couldn't bring herself to look at him. "Embezzlement."

In desperation, Linc addressed his employer. "Mr. Bradford, you have to listen to me. This woman is crazy. I'm an accountant. A number cruncher. I write checks and balance accounts. That's it, I swear."

"I hope that's the case," Kent said with surprising equanimity. "But I think we'll examine some of those checks and accounts to be on the safe side."

Harry stepped forward and held out his hand. "I believe that's my cue to introduce myself. The name's Jones. I guess you could say I'm the man who watches out for Bradford. I make sure no one pulls any nasty tricks with his money. I'm also the person who gets to take them down if they try." He bared his teeth. "Fair warning. When I take them down, they stay down."

Linc's eyes widened. "Jones? Harry Jones?" He stumbled to his feet and backed rapidly away, regarding Harry's hand as though he'd offered a fistful of razor-sharp claws.

It was then Madison knew. Her cousin was guilty as hell. She also knew something far worse. Harry was every bit as intimidating as he'd always claimed. Ever since she'd been trapped on the elevator with him, she'd foolishly tried to deny his innate power. She was probably the only person in the entire world who hadn't recognized it at first sight. Even Rosy understood his dominance. She just chose to contend with it in her own unique fashion.

Madison closed her eyes. She'd called Harry a lion almost from the first, but she hadn't believed it, not really. That was why he'd insisted she accompany him. He wanted her to see him for what he truly was. A predator. A man who went for the throat with a ferocious ease that could only come from years of practice. Confronting that truth didn't change how she felt about him. But it might change how he felt about her, especially once he learned the rest of her background.

"I gather you've heard of me." Harry addressed Linc. "This will make our discussion much easier."

"My uncle warned me—" Her cousin broke off abruptly as he realized what he'd been about to say. "I'd like to call him, if you don't mind."

"You need a criminal attorney, not an accountant," Madison said gently. "Don't bother with Dad. I suggest you call Uncle Tyler."

She couldn't take any more. Not only was one of her closest relatives involved in a nasty case of embezzlement, but her father had probably helped. At the very least he would have advised her cousin every inch of the way. And there was another part of this whole horrible incident that distressed her, a piece of her past that she couldn't bring herself to face.

Without a word, she turned and left the office. She didn't stop once outside. The brisk tap-tap of her pumps echoed off the walls, the sound quickening with each step as she bolted toward the entrance to Bradford's.

Shoving open the door, she pelted down the stairs leading to the walkway as swiftly as her heels would allow. She had no idea where she was headed. She simply knew she had to get as far away from Linc and the memories he'd resurrected as she could.

She never heard Harry coming. One minute she was racing down the walkway and the next an ironlike arm yanked her to a stop and spun her around. "Where are you going?" he demanded.

"I don't know. I don't care." Her words came in swift, frantic pants. "Anywhere that's not here."

"Why? Don't you realize how helpful you've been? If you're right about Linc, you've probably saved Kent's company. Or at least a good chunk of it."

"Dammit, Harry! Don't you understand? His name isn't Linc Smith. It's Adams. Lincoln Adams. And he's family, my cousin to be exact."

"I'm sorry, Madison." Compassion vied with ruthless intent. "You know that doesn't change what has to be done."

He still didn't get it. "Of course, I know. That's only one of the reasons I'm upset."

"What's the other?"

She pointed a shaky finger toward Bradford's and said the words that would damn her in his eyes. "I'm part of all that. That could have been me."

"What the hell are you talking about?" Shards of green appeared in his eyes, warning of his anger. "You're not like him. You never could be. I may not have known you long, but I've learned that much about you. I can understand if you don't want to help take him down, but—"

She tugged free of his grasp. "No! You don't understand."

"Then explain it to me."

"I can't. Not here. Not like this. Not when—" Her voice broke and she fought to regain control. "Not when my cousin is waiting for you to stalk in there and rip him to shreds."

Harry's face emptied of expression. "Is that what I'm going to do?"

"It's the nature of lions, isn't it?" It was a statement of fact, one neither of them could deny.

"Yes, I suppose it is."

"Just like it's the nature of snakes to strike when cornered."

"Is that a warning?"

"Absolutely. Linc's no match for you, but the people who put him up to this will do everything in their power to protect him." She shivered. "And they have a lot of power."

"I'll be sure to watch my back."

"And Kent's, too." She swiped at her cheeks and forced herself to give Harry the information he'd need to finish his job. It was the least she could do under the circumstances. "If you want to recover some of the money, I suggest you check for customer accounts that have similar names. Like Sheffield Manufacturing and Sheffield Marketing. Inexperienced auditors don't always catch the duplication because they think it's two separate divisions of the same company. But one will be legit and the other bogus. Linc will have syphoned off company money by making payments based on falsified invoices to the bogus firm. You might also check to see if any product has been sent to them. He may have a black market operation going, as well. Though I'm hoping he hasn't had time to get that started yet."

To her relief, Harry didn't ask how she knew. "At least stay until I wrap things up here."

"I can't." She couldn't face Linc again. Not after what had happened, not when so much of it was her fault. "Don't worry, Harry. I'm not Aunt Dell. I have a lot of practice finding my way home."

He must have recognized her determination because he didn't argue further. "Okay, Madison. Go, if that's what you want. But this discussion isn't over. Not by a long shot."

"I'm well aware of that." She turned to leave, then remembered one last thing. "Don't forget to get the games Rosy requested."

"Those games are the least of my worries."

"They won't be if you forget. You'll never hear the end of it." She continued to hesitate. "You might also consider introducing Kent to Rosy."

"You have got to be kidding me!" He'd thoroughly lost his temper this time. "All hell is breaking loose and you're matchmaking?"

She shrugged. "Maybe some good can come out of it. It would help—" Her voice broke again and she knew she had to leave before she fell apart altogether.

"Honey, please. Stay."

"I can't."

"Then promise me you'll come by the hotel later this evening."

"I'll try. If not, I'll see you at the office tomorrow." She suddenly remembered and her pain magnified. "That's right. We're finished with everything, aren't we?"

"We're not finished," Harry retorted. "Not by a long shot."

"Somehow," she whispered, "I suspect we are."

CHAPTER NINE

Principle 9: Sex is Good...
Making Love is Better.

THE setting sun had just kissed the Olympic Mountains when Madison entered Harry's high-rise hotel. She took the elevator straight to the top and walked to the door of his suite. Her palms were damp from nerves and she brushed them against her thighs. She should have changed before coming. Her salmon-colored suit jacket and skirt, which had been crisp and jaunty this morning, had definitely wilted. But as much as she'd appreciate any excuse to turn tail and run, she couldn't. She owed Harry better than that. Not giving herself time to reconsider, she balled up her fist and banged on the door. It opened before she could do more than take a single, steadying breath.

Harry stood there and he didn't appear happy. She couldn't decide whether the unnaturally rumpled state of his hair tipped her off to that fact, or if it was the way his tie hung slightly askew. Or maybe it was the steam pouring out of his ears and the half-crazed expression in his eyes that clued her in. Yeah, that was probably it.

"Lady, you are in one hell of a lot of trouble," he announced. Snatching her into his arms, he carried her over the threshold, slamming the door behind them with a single savage kick.

149

"Have you lost your mind?" She struggled in vain against his unyielding strength. "Put me down!"

"Have I lost *my* mind?" The question rumbled through her, reverberating with anger and frustration and— And could it be fear? It didn't seem possible considering the source. "That's rich, coming from you."

"What are you talking about?"

He strode into the living room and dumped her onto her feet. Then he seized her purse and briefcase from one of the chairs and shook them at her. "I'm talking about these. You left them at Bradford's when you bolted. As soon as I realized you'd forgotten them, I scoured every inch of the city looking for you. Do you have any idea how worried I've been, imagining you wandering around trying to find a way home without money or a cell phone at your disposal?"

"Oh." She shrugged. "I called a cab."

Her explanation did little to appease him. Tension crackled like electricity, filling the air with threat. "And you paid for that...how?"

She wouldn't let him browbeat her. Planting her hands on her hips, she faced him down. "I have a tab with all the local companies. Aunt Dell gets lost so often it seemed like the most logical solution to the problem. Not that this is any of your business. In case you didn't notice, I'm a grown woman, Harry. I can take care of myself."

"If today's an example of you taking care of yourself, I suggest you reevaluate your criteria." He paced in front of her, the words exploding from him. "What the *hell* were you thinking, Madison? You've never gone longer than two minutes without a cell phone glued to your ear. No one at the office knew where you were. The Sunflowers were in a flat-out panic."

The Sunflowers or Harry? She didn't have the nerve to ask. "I guess I should have called you, but I needed time to think." She slipped further into the room. If she gave Harry a wide berth it wasn't deliberate, she told herself. There were just certain parts of the room she felt more comfortable occupying, all of which kept her as far from a pair of unsheathed claws as possible. It certainly had nothing to do with the tension clinging to him, or the way he paced in perfect imitation of a caged lion. "And I did phone Rosy. I told her to let you know that I'd be over later this evening. I can't help it if she kept the information from you."

His strides ate up the generous-size room. "Remind me to have words with that girl." He stabbed the air with his finger. "And not just about her lack of communication skills. She's pushed me as far as I intend to be pushed today."

Madison regarded him warily. "What else has she done?"

"Aside from failing to pass on your message, she broke into my hotel room and redecorated the place."

He swept his arm toward the dining room. From where she stood, Madison could see that the table had been set for two, crystal and silver gleaming, blood-red candlesticks awaiting the strike of a match. Instead of the floral centerpiece that had been there on her last visit, an oddly shaped bush squatted in the middle of the table. Okay, so Rosy probably shouldn't have entered without permission, but this didn't look too terrible. Certainly not anything to get annoyed about.

"You might be right about my family trying their hand at a little matchmaking," Madison conceded. "I guess Rosy decided to set the stage once she found out I planned to drop by."

"You think?" He thrust a hand through his hair. "She also brought dinner."

"And that's a bad thing, I gather?"

"You tell me. Apparently dinner in Rosy's world consists solely of chocolate, honey and whipped cream."

"Oh, dear."

"With instructions."

Uh-oh. "Instructions?"

"How-to instructions," he clarified. "According to Rosy, I need educating on the proper way to—how did she put it? Oh, right. 'Successfully install my hard drive.' And just as a side note, you can forget about setting her up with Kent. If you think I'm going to let her anywhere near him, you're crazy. I'm not about to have him corrupted by that sex-crazed lunatic. He's a nice kid. You should read some of the kinky stuff she put in that message."

Madison blushed. There were a few facts about her cousin she'd rather not know. "Harry—"

"I'm not finished. Not by a long shot. Not only did she arrange for our dinner, but she put *things* in my bed."

"What sort of things?" Madison asked cautiously.

"Flowery things." If matters weren't so serious, she'd have laughed at his outraged expression. "Petals and herbs that will no doubt end up in places no petal or herb belongs. And if that's not enough to chase you away, she brought along a tree."

Her gaze returned to the shrub decorating the table. "Rosy left that for you?"

"No. Rosy left it for *you.* A 'naughty-but-safe' tree with leaves made out of very interesting foil packets in every color and style imaginable."

"Every size, too?" The question escaped before she could utilize an iota of common sense.

"No. Only one." Brilliant green lights appeared in his eyes, warning that she'd be wise to keep any future smart-mouthed remarks to herself. "Fortunately, Rosy seems to have more confidence in that regard than you. We're talking about a tree covered in nice, big oak leaves. Not a single scrawny pine needle in sight."

Heaven help her! She wouldn't get *that* image out of her head anytime soon. She scrambled to stay focused. "I'm sorry Rosy upset you. I'll have a talk with her first thing tomorrow."

He stopped pacing, pausing a scant few feet away. "She's not the one who upset me. She's the one I'm taking my temper out on so I don't go after the real culprit."

It didn't take much brainpower to figure out who he meant. "Me."

"You. And I don't mean your disappearing act. That's just part of it."

"Then what?"

"I'm talking about the way you've been shying away from developing a relationship with me and your fear of commitment. I'm talking about your reaction to what happened at Bradford's today. And I'm talking about how you run at the first sign of anyone getting too close." He folded his arms across his chest and fixed her with his lion's stare. "What's going on, Madison? Explain it to me."

She took a deep breath. No more ducking the issue. Harry deserved total honesty and that's what she'd give him, no matter how much it hurt. "I don't think it's working out between us."

"Why?"

The single, razor-sharp word tipped her off that his emotions still ran hot and passionate, despite his current air of calm. She crossed to the window and swept aside the drapes, fabricating an intense interest in the view. Not that the cityscape made much impression. She was too keenly aware of the man standing behind her to focus on anything else. "We're too different."

"This is because of Linc, isn't it?"

"My cousin doesn't have anything to do with my decision. He simply brought home certain facts."

"Like what?"

"Like..." She risked a quick glance over her shoulder. The lion had stalked closer and she inched to one side. "Like we come from worlds that have nothing in common."

He matched her movements, shifting positions just enough to keep her on edge, while at the same time managing to block all avenues of retreat. She swiveled to face him. It was utterly unfair that he was so large, she silently stewed. An average-size man wouldn't have been able to get away with those sorts of tactics.

"I'd say we had a lot in common," Harry argued.

"You're wrong."

"Am I? Let's see..." He reached for his tie, ripping at the knot. "We're both practical."

She lifted her chin with a touch of defiance, pretending not to notice his actions, pretending even harder not to be unnerved by them. "I recently discovered that I'm nowhere near as practical as I once thought. Now that I think about it, I haven't acted with any practicality at all these last couple of weeks."

The tie came free and he tossed it aside without a second glance. "We both excel at business."

"You mean *you* excel at business. Apparently, I excel at *playing* at business."

He continued as though she hadn't interrupted, tugging at the buttons of his shirt as he spoke. "We both have a knack for telling people what to do with their money."

"Don't you dare pretend we're in the same category," she stormed. "If my father knows who you are that means you're big. Very big."

"I warned you about that right from the start." She found the gentleness of his tone disconcerting, perhaps because it was at direct odds with the fierceness of his gaze. "If you chose not to believe me, I can't be held responsible. And while we're on the subject of choosing what to believe and what not to, need I mention the word 'intimidation'? I seem to remember telling you I'd been called that on more than one occasion, too."

"Don't remind me. I knew you were a lion the first time I saw you," she complained. "I should have trusted my instincts from the beginning."

"Why didn't you?"

"Because by then we'd— In the elevator I'd— You'd—" She released her breath in an exasperated huff. "You know what I mean. It was very unfair of you to kiss me like you were a normal person and then turn around and be someone else when the lights came on."

"I was trying to reassure you, not mislead you." He'd finished with the buttons lining his shirt and glanced down to remove his cufflinks. They were heavy nuggets of misshapen gold and he discarded them onto a nearby coffee table as though they were cheap bits of plastic. "The reason you ignored the truth was because you didn't want to face the ramifications."

"What ramifications?"

"That you'd caught a lion by the tail and didn't quite know what to do with him."

"Well, I do now," she retorted. "I'm setting him free."

"Too late, sweetheart." He released his belt and ripped the leather through the loops. It cracked like a whip, the sound splitting the heaviness of the air around them. "You're stuck with him, teeth, claws, hungry roar and all."

Her breathing kicked up a notch. "Why are you doing this? Why can't you accept that it's not working out between us and let it go?"

"Let you go, you mean."

"Yes!"

"Not a chance." He tore the shirt from his shoulders and dropped it to the floor. With a single stride he ate up the final few feet separating them. Everything about him felt intensely male, overwhelmingly male. His partial nudity, his distinctive scent, the endless ripple of muscle that eclipsed all else within sight, the tough, ravenous timbre of his voice. Even the earthy glitter in his eyes held a masculine threat. "Admit it, Madison, you want me as much as I want you."

"Do you need to hear me admit it? Fine. I want you. I'd like to have you in my bed for a night or two of mindless sex. And then I'd like to say thank you very much and wave a fond farewell."

"That's all this is? Lust?"

She didn't have a single qualm about admitting it. "That's all," she confirmed.

"And a few nights of mindless sex will suffice. Appetite satisfied?"

"No question."

"So what are you waiting for?" He touched her, a

single sweep of his finger that scorched her skin from jawline to collarbone. "There's a bedroom a few feet away. Rosy's naughty-but-safe tree has dozens of leaves to choose from. All you have to do is pick one. That is what you asked for, isn't it?"

"Yes."

It was the truth. She'd wanted him from the first minute his voice had filled her ears. Maybe she'd been affected by those stupid love principles of Bartholomew's, after all. But somehow she questioned that it was that simple. She and Harry had connected on the elevator. And no matter how much she tried to deny it, they were more alike than not. But that didn't mean they were destined to share forever together. Her future didn't offer such a dream. Still... They had tonight, didn't they?

"Harry," she whispered. "You asked if we could have an affair."

He tried to read her expression, to analyze precisely where she was going with her declaration. "Are you agreeing?"

"Yes."

He took an educated guess. "But it'll be a temporary relationship, right?"

"No commitment. No promises. Just two people who crave each other," she confirmed.

Why didn't that surprise him? "Are you sure that's all there is to it?"

"I'm positive." His hesitation must have bothered her because an urgency gathered in her voice. "Please, Harry. Make love to me."

Love? "I thought you said sex."

She stared in confusion. "I did."

He inclined his head. "Then that's what I'll give you."

His mouth came down on hers, ending any further discussion. His touch was hard and driven and purposeful, and she surrendered to him without hesitation or doubt. He removed her suit jacket in a few swift movements, before making short work of the buttons anchoring both her skirt and blouse. Within seconds he'd stripped her of those, as well. And in between the loss of each garment he continued to take her mouth in short, biting kisses.

"Is this what you want?" he demanded.

"Yes. Oh, yes."

His hands sank deep into her hair, releasing the pent-up curls as easily as he'd released her desire. Streams of dark ringlets poured over her shoulders to rest against the upper curves of her breasts. "No strings," he told her. "No emotional attachment. Just raw sex."

She stirred at that and he stole any objections in a searing kiss that mated mouth and tongue and breath. If he only had a single night with her, he wanted to know all of her. And he wanted Madison to know all of him, as well. But not quite yet. She wasn't ready for that. She'd asked for something far different and he'd give it to her right up until she discovered her mistake.

Reaching behind her, he released her bra. It fell away and he cupped her breasts. They were full and sweet and richly crested and they tempted him beyond restraint. Slowly he lowered his head and kissed each tip, deliberately driving the peaks into tightly furled buds of sensation. A shudder raced through her and her breath quickened, but she didn't protest.

"More?" he asked.

She didn't appear capable of uttering a single word. Instead, she nodded with unmistakable urgency.

Dropping to one knee, he removed the last of her

clothing, drawing her panties from her hips. He followed the scrap of silk and lace down the length of her legs with slow, deliberate strokes designed to arouse. She shuddered at each caress, quivering as his touch grew bolder, his exploration more intimate. He swept his hands up the inside of her thighs, finding the hot, moist core of her, feeling her flower to full ripeness against his fingers.

She tugged at him, pulling him upward. "Please, Harry. I can't wait any longer."

"Not yet. Touch me first, Madison," he demanded. "Show me that I'm the one you need tonight. The only one. Or will any man do?"

She shuddered at the order, reaching for him with notable hesitation. Her fingers slid across his chest, making shallow furrows in his hair as she explored each ridge and hollow. With a barely audible sigh she leaned into him, her softness a stark counterpoint to his harder form. She pressed her lips against the base of his throat in a damp, openmouthed kiss and reached for the opening of his trousers. The zip parted beneath her fingers. And then she was inside.

"It's you I want, Harry. Only you."

His breath rushed from his lungs in a silent groan. He'd always prided himself on his control, but with that simple, tentative touch, she nearly unmanned him. He'd planned to give her what she'd requested until she stopped him. No emotion, no fairy-tale romance. Just a man and a woman and the elemental desire that drove them to seek each other out. But he couldn't keep going. He was too close to the edge, too close to taking her with the heartless disregard she'd requested. If that happened, they'd both regret it afterward. They'd end up feeling cheated, the memories uncomfortable rather than unforgettable. He knew that, even if she didn't. Gathering the remaining shreds of his willpower, he decided to end this before it went too far.

"Go pick a leaf, Madison." His words escaped in a guttural demand. "Let's get down to business."

"Business?" Her eyes opened, a momentary confusion shadowing the passion. "What are you talking about, Harry?"

"I'm talking about getting on with it." He dropped a hard kiss on her mouth. "Should I find Rosy's instructions? Would that help? There are a few things on there that might be new to you. And how about the honey? Or do you prefer chocolate and whipped cream?"

"No. No, of course not." Her brow wrinkled. "I don't understand. What are you doing?"

"I'm giving you what you asked for, remember? Sex. Hot, mindless, can't-remember-your-name-in-the-morning sex." He infused a hint of impatience in his voice. "Come on, sweetheart. What's the holdup? There's a bed waiting. Leaves to pluck. And dinner to eat off each other. What more could you want?"

She shook her head, her confusion growing, eclipsing all other emotion. "Stop it, Harry. I don't like this. You're making it sound so...so—"

"Sordid?"

She shivered and glanced around as though suddenly aware of where they were and what they were doing. Her arms folded around herself like a flower closing against the uncomfortable chill of nightfall. "This has been a mistake. I think I should go home."

"You're right. This is a mistake." Ever so carefully, he drew her into his arms, holding her with a tenderness she couldn't mistake. "Let me show you why."

Harry didn't give her a chance to protest, but kissed

her once more. Only this time, he gave her all she'd rejected before. He made love to her mouth with slow, deep, hungry kisses. She felt stiff in his arms at first. But with each kiss, she relaxed a little more, opening to him, encouraging him with disjointed pleas and urgent hands. And this time when he touched her it was with more than the desire to arouse. He made their pairing a benediction.

He worshiped her body, telling her without words what he felt and how it should be between them. With each stroke and kiss and caress, he showed her the difference between what she'd requested and what she truly wanted. And he gave to her with unstinting generosity. Her response was all he hoped for and more. She said the words he couldn't, gifting him with whispered secrets he'd always treasure. Where before her lovemaking was hesitant and unsure, now it was certain and tender, her surrender one of total abandon.

"Is this what you want?" he asked again.

"Yes. Oh, yes."

"Sex?"

"No." She cupped his face, smoothing his jaw with her thumbs, her eyes filled with apology. "I'm sorry, Harry. I was wrong before. I didn't understand. Make love to me. Please."

He didn't need to hear any more. Sweeping her into his arms he headed for the bedroom, sidetracking only long enough for Madison to pluck one of the colorful leaves from the tree in the dining room. Once in the bedroom, he settled her onto the mattress. The scent of flowers and crushed herbs wrapping around them in lush welcome, the effect more stimulating than he'd have thought possible.

"Remind me to thank Rosy," he muttered, following her onto the bed.

"Thank her? I thought you planned to kill her."

"First I'll thank her, after that I'll kill her."

She wrapped herself around him and her hands chased a nerve-racking path from his chest to his abdomen before drifting lower. "Oh, dear." Her hands stilled. "Harry?"

He stifled a groan. "What's wrong now?" he managed to ask.

"I'll have to tell Rosy to forget about the oak leaves next time."

"Don't tell me we need pine needles, after all?"

She tugged him down on top of her. "Not pine needles. We're going to need palm fronds. Great big palm fronds."

And then there was no more talking, other than the murmured words that fully expressed their moment of joining. They were soft words, like the gentlest of caresses. They were demanding, like the driving need that thrust them together. They were pleading, like the slow, urgent climb toward completion. And they were exultant, like the fierce tumble into ecstasy.

Harry swept the curls from Madison's face, holding her in the aftermath of a moment unlike any he'd ever known before. Where once she'd demanded an emotionless mating, now she wept from a pleasure that could have only come from a joining that transcended the physical act itself. Instead of the temporary link she'd planned to fashion, an unbreakable bond had been forged. Whether she realized it or not, she'd committed herself to him.

And he wasn't about to let her go.

* * *

Madison wasn't sure how long she slept. But it was the most peaceful night she'd ever known. Harry's generosity had been beyond belief. She'd asked for an evening of passion and he'd offered so much more. The passion, yes. But he'd given it depth and validity by making love to her.

Her breath caught. *Making love.* The words had the unmistakable ring of truth to them. How could she have been such a fool? What they'd shared hadn't been a one-night stand or a casual affair. There'd been a permanence in their joining. When he'd taken her it had been with love, a love that had its core deep inside, their feelings for each other inexorably joined whether she'd been willing to admit it or not. But Harry had known. And he'd forced her to lower her guard and allow him close enough to recognize the truth of what they'd experienced.

She glanced over at him. He sprawled across the mattress with all the indolent grace of a sated lion and she turned to him for reassurance, the physical bond that united them every bit as powerful and unbreakable as the emotional. She froze at the last moment, alarmed by her instinctive actions. Had their connection really grown so strong in just one night?

Silently, she escaped the bed and crossed to the window. Far below, Seattle slept. At least, it slept as much as any large city could. Lights flickered and cars moved along streets laid out in tidy grids. But there was a languid, sleepy quality about the scene, as though time had slowed. She leaned her forehead against the cool glass and faced the unavoidable truth. *She'd fallen in love with Harry.* What the devil was she going to do now?

''Sweetheart?'' Harry came up behind and wrapped a

sheet around her, securing it with his arms. "What's wrong?"

She sank into his embrace, reveling in everything about him—his strength, his solidness, his caring. His love. "I'm a fool."

He smiled tenderly. "Why? Because you didn't recognize what we shared as soon as I did?"

"Yes. I thought I could keep it casual. That we could get through this without anyone getting hurt."

"Get *through* it?" He shook his head in exasperation. "You act like this is a sickness or an accident to be endured and then thrown off. Don't you get it? I don't just want your body. I want you. All of you. Your heart and soul, as well as your body."

"Harry—"

"No, Madison. Don't interrupt." He cupped her close, locking her into perfect alignment against him. "I'm talking marriage here, honey. Permanence. I mean ring on the finger, a horde of kids overrunning the homestead, growing old together, rocking chairs on the porch sort of permanence. The whole enchilada. I want to start at once-upon-a-time with you and go straight through until we reach happily-ever-after."

They were the sort of words a woman waited her entire life to hear. And they hurt more than she'd thought possible. "No, you don't. I'm not the woman you think I am."

He pressed his mouth to the top of her head and she leaned into him, her cheek resting close to the steady, dependable beat of his heart. "You're everything I imagined and more," he assured her.

"Harry—" she tried again.

"My turn first, Madison. Before we discuss the future,

there's something I have to tell you. Something I've kept from you.''

"That makes two of us," she murmured.

He didn't seem to hear. "I'd have told you right up front, but Sunny asked me to hold off."

"It's clear I need to have a talk with that woman."

"Actually, I would have told you at lunch that very first day, but lunch never happened because Dad's signing ran long. Then there was the incident on the elevator and you said all those things about the book. When Sunny and my father found out how you felt, they asked me to wait until you'd read the damn thing and realized it wasn't some sort of love manual like you thought."

She pulled back slightly. "What in the world are you talking about?"

He took a deep breath. "Screw it. Next time I'm listening to my instincts and the hell with tact." He cupped her face, tilting her chin so she could see his expression in the soft glow of the city lights. She'd witnessed that fierce determination before. It had gleamed in his eyes right before he'd ripped into her cousin. "The truth is, I wrote *The Principles of Love,* not my father."

CHAPTER TEN

Principle 10: Trust your instincts
and take a chance...
If you think the person might be right for you,
go for it. Don't let fear or hesitation
come between you and true love.

IT TOOK a full minute for Harry's words to sink in. The instant they had, Madison fought free of his arms. "You wrote the book," she echoed.

"Yes."

She retreated, the distancing part physical and part emotional. Hugging the sheet close, she regarded him warily. "Then why is your father taking credit for it?"

"I asked him to."

"I don't understand."

He crossed the room and grabbed a pair of jeans from the dresser. "I'm an economist, Madison. I deal with facts and figures. Who the hell is going to give credence to a book about romantic rules written by a financial analyst?" He thrust his legs into the jeans and yanked them over his hips. "Nor am I a salesman. I can't sit around a bookstore and spend my day smiling and shaking hands. Aside from the fact that I'd go insane, I have a business to run. A business I spent years building."

"But your father can sit around in your place, is that it?"

"He loves meeting people. He's a born socializer. And he believes in my book."

"Don't you?"

He shrugged. "Sure. I just don't think it deserves all the attention it's gotten. To be honest, it started as something to take my mind off work. Thoughts I'd jot down when I was flying from one part of the country to the other. When I finally ran out of ideas, I e-mailed the whole mess to Dad. I thought he'd get a chuckle out of his sensible son writing a book about the principles of love. Instead he organized what I'd written into manuscript form and sent it off to an agent. I didn't even find out what he'd done until he slapped the contract on my desk. So I guess you could say he co-authored the book. He certainly expended more time and effort on it than I did."

"Why didn't you tell me the truth right away?"

"And when would that have been?" He snapped his fingers. "Oh, I remember. I should have said something when you first got on the elevator and were in the middle of trashing my book. That would have been the perfect opportunity to confess the truth, right?"

His sarcasm stung. "I can't help it if I didn't like what you'd written."

"Didn't like it?" he repeated in a dangerous voice. "Didn't *like* it? 'Total twaddle. Bilge, drivel, malarkey, not to mention poppycock.' Those were your exact words, Madison, after you'd read...what? A whole three pages? That didn't exactly inspire me to confess the truth."

She started to plant her hands on her hips, only remembering the sheet at the last possible minute. Wrapping the length around herself several times, she tossed the trailing end over one shoulder. No doubt she looked like a bedraggled mummy, but that couldn't be helped. It was better than having the sheet—not to mention her dignity—puddled on the floor around her ankles. "I'm sorry if I offended you, but I can't be the only person in the universe who doesn't like the idea of some sex manual telling me how to get a man into my bed."

"Why should you when telling him 'I want a night of mindless sex' works so well?"

"*Oh!* That is *so* low."

"About as low as calling my book a sex manual. For the last time, they're just simple principles on how to forge strong male-female relationships, not a how-to instruction book." Anger glittered in his eyes and he paced in front of her. He hadn't bothered to fasten his jeans and they gaped threateningly with each stride. "If you'd taken more than two minutes to read the damn thing, you'd know that. But you made up your mind before you even cracked the cover, didn't you?"

She lifted her chin. "My mistake. Maybe if I had read it I'd have recognized your principles in action. I assume that's what the past few weeks have been about? Putting your theory to the test? Or am I the sequel?"

It was the wrong thing to say. For a minute she thought he'd explode, his temper as close to the edge as she'd ever seen it. But his control proved phenomenal. "Honey, so far our relationship doesn't live up to the original, let alone a sequel." He waited for that to impact before continuing. "Let's get on with it, Madison."

"What do you mean?"

"I mean go ahead. You're dying to accuse me of something unethical." He swept his hand through the air in a mocking bow. "Say it. Say it so you have an excuse to run away."

"I'm not looking for an excuse to run away!" She

glared at him. "Okay, maybe a little. But I don't think for one minute that you're unethical. You're the most honorable man I've ever met. And trust me, I've seen enough of the other sort to know the difference."

She hadn't appeased him. He rubbed a hand across the back of his neck, his expression one of utter disgust. "As much as I appreciate your ringing endorsement, we wouldn't be having this discussion if I'd followed my own principles."

"Why not?" she asked before she could stop herself.

"Principle number seven will answer that question. Feel free to read up on it."

"I don't suppose you'd care to give me a hint?"

"It deals with honesty and integrity. Something I forgot these past couple of weeks. But I guarantee I won't forget again." He took a deep breath, his determination unmistakable. "All right, Madison. What do you say we deal with the real problem?"

"Which is?"

"You're looking for any reason to get out of the commitment we made last night. You're running scared. And by not telling you about the book, I've handed you the perfect excuse to back away from a relationship with me."

He was right, which only served to make her angrier. "You want honesty? Fine. I *am* running scared. It's taking everything I have to keep standing here arguing with you. If I could get my clothes on without dropping this sheet, I'd be out of here like a shot. There. How's that for honesty?"

His mouth twitched, a momentary amusement overriding his anger. "Pretty damned honest. I think I'll make a point of hiding your clothes every time we have a fight."

Every time. The words suggested they had a future and that was all it took to send her into a panic. She took a hasty step backward, tripping over the sheet and almost losing her balance. Her actions impacted with devastating force. For a brief instant his eyes burned a brilliant green before going blank, like one of heaven's stars winking out of existence. Without a word, he disappeared from the bedroom, returning a minute later with her clothing in hand.

"Here." He tossed her suit and underclothes onto the bed. "I think we've said all that's necessary."

Turning his back on her, he left the room, closing the door behind him. Madison didn't waste any time. Dropping the sheet, she yanked on her clothes with quick, economical movements. As soon as she'd finished, she escaped into the living room. Harry waited for her, his emotions hidden behind his most intimidating business mask.

She stood in the middle of the room and struggled to find the right words. "Could you at least tell me whether all this has been a setup?"

"You mean last night?"

"That's part of it. But I really mean you and me."

"Yes, we were a setup."

She moistened her lips. "Was I also some sort of experiment?" she forced herself to ask.

Harry hesitated for a minute before shaking his head. "I think that's for you to decide." He turned and walked to the window. Resting his forearm against the glass, he stared out at the city. "It's time for you to go, Madison."

"Harry—"

"Don't feel bad, sweetheart." He cut her off. "I took

a chance and it didn't work out. But at least I tried. Principle number ten, in case you're interested.''

She hesitated. When he didn't make any move to turn around, she gathered up her purse and briefcase and crossed to the suite door. He was right. She was using their argument as an excuse to run. And with each step that took her further from him, a voice in her head screamed for her to stop. To go to him and tell him how she felt. To reveal what had happened to her those years she'd spent with her father. To explain why she found it so difficult to trust or to commit to someone. But it was a story she hadn't told another living soul, not even the Sunflowers, and she couldn't bring herself to start telling it now.

So instead of following her heart, she walked steadily toward purgatory.

Madison opened the door to her office, exhaustion dogging her every step of the way. For some reason the lights were out and she automatically flicked them on.

"Surprise!"

Sunflowers overflowed her office, every last one decked out in party hats and blowing toy horns. For a minute, Madison could only stand with her mouth gaping, staring in stunned disbelief. Her birthday! Good heavens. She'd forgotten all about it. She gazed at her family, took in the broad smiles and happy faces and promptly burst into tears. Pandemonium resulted, her relatives swarming around her.

"What's wrong?"

"What happened?"

Rosy groaned. "Harry! What is it with men and following simple, basic instructions? They get to the part that says 'Insert Flap A into Slot B' and they totally lose it.''

Madison shook her head, fighting for control. "No, you're wrong. It's not that. Linc. Dad—" The tears came harder, preventing her from explaining.

Sunny fluttered to her side, wrapping her up in a warm hug. "There, there, precious. Tell your grandmother all about it. What's happened?"

"I blew it," she managed to say. "With Harry. I really, truly blew it."

"But he was our birthday present to you," Rosy complained. A disgruntled expression crossed her face. "Oh, I get it. I should have left instructions for *you* instead of *him.*"

"Quiet, Rosy," Daniel ordered. "This is important. Could everyone please excuse us? I'd like to handle things from here."

Sunny looked alarmed. "I don't know. This might require a woman's touch."

Determination settled on his face. "I can do it. I haven't been very good at helping people in the past. But I'm positive I can help Madison. Give me a chance to try."

For the first time within Madison's memory, no one argued. Daniel waited while everyone exited the office, dejected balloons, streamers and party hats trailing in their wake. As soon as they were alone, he shut the door and approached. He tugged a crumpled manila envelope from his back pocket.

Madison glanced at it curiously, wiping tears from her cheeks. "What's that, Uncle Daniel?"

"It's your birthday present." His brows drew together. "I wasn't sure I should give it to you. I'd hoped I could help get you and Harry together using the principles like everyone else planned to and make that my gift. But I couldn't figure out how to do it.''

''Trust me, I don't mind.''

He smiled. ''No, I suppose not. And I doubt I'd have done a very good job, even if I'd had the opportunity to try.'' A frown overtook his smile. ''But I really wanted to help.''

''Thank you. It means the world to me that you've all been so kind. Not just with Harry.'' Tears threatened again. ''You all accepted me when I needed you most.''

''No thanks necessary. We were thrilled to have you return home. And you've done so much for us over the years that I've been racking my brain to come up with some way to show you how grateful we are. So...'' He fingered the envelope, finally holding it out. ''Here.''

''What is it?''

''It's the real reason Harry came to Seattle.''

''The real reason?'' Madison regarded the envelope as if it were disaster in the making. ''Which real reason? As a favor to Sunny? To take a look at our financial situation? Or was it in response to the Sunflowers matchmaking attempts?''

''None of the above.'' When she didn't take the envelope, he set it gently on her desk. ''It's all in there. Why he came. Why he stayed. And why he's the perfect man for you.''

Curiosity won over hesitation and she picked up the envelope. Breaking the seal, she pulled out the papers. It only took an instant to realize what she held. ''Oh, no. Please tell me this isn't what I think it is.''

''They're pages from your journal. Rosy sent them to Bartholomew.''

Tears glittered in her eyes once again. ''Why would she do such a thing?''

"Because she thought he'd like to have the information for a possible sequel to his book." He shrugged apologetically. "She was wrong, of course. Wrong to send it. And wrong to think either Bartholomew or Harry would use it for personal gain."

Her head jerked up as the full significance of his words sank in. "You know about Harry?"

"That he wrote *The Principles?* Sure. I figured it out the second time I read the book. It sounded just like him. How about you?"

"I...I haven't read it, yet."

He nodded as though it confirmed his suspicions. "Maybe you should. You might realize that your practical, logical—not to mention intimidating—economist is a romantic at heart. Otherwise what other reason would he have to come rushing out here once he'd read your blueprint for the perfect man?"

She looked down at the copies of her most private thoughts and dreams and shook her head. "I don't understand. Why would he come in response to this?"

"I haven't read what you wrote." He blushed. "Private, you know. But at a guess, there was something he read there that made him think the two of you would be compatible."

"You're wrong. You have to be wrong. He came because Sunny asked him. Because Bartholomew—"

Daniel simply fixed her with a gaze of absolute, unquestioning conviction.

"How do you know?" she pleaded. "How can you be so certain?"

"All I can tell you is that Bartholomew faxed him the pages from your journal and within five minutes Harry dropped everything and was on the next plane to Seattle. And he's stayed here, neglecting multi-million-dollar clients so that he could spend time with you.'' He patted her hand. ''Somehow I doubt it has anything to do with the Sunflowers, our financial situation, or his book.''

''But I haven't told him about—''

''About your past?''

Her chin wobbled alarmingly. ''There are things I haven't even told any of you,'' she whispered. ''Terrible things.''

Daniel released his breath in a long sigh. ''Do you know what today is?''

''My birthday.''

He dropped his hands onto her shoulders. ''It's more than that, Madison. It's the day you decided to change your life. We can guess how hard your choice was and what it cost you. Why do you think we make such a big deal over your birthdays each year?''

They knew. The Sunflowers knew her secret. She fought to breathe. ''How long?'' she demanded in a strangled voice. ''How long have you all known?''

''From the beginning. Your father made sure we were told.''

''And you still took me in?'' She couldn't believe it.

''Of course we did. You're family. We're always there for each other, no matter how much trouble we're in.'' He gave her a quick hug. ''Which brings us to your problem with Harry. I assume your current woes are because you haven't told him the truth.''

''I couldn't. I just couldn't.''

''Don't you trust him?''

''Of course I do.'' The words escaped without volition. And they came straight from the heart. ''Yes. Yes, I do. I trust him with my life.''

''Ah.'' He nodded sagely. ''That explains why you're here with us, instead of with him.''

The truth hit with devastating force. She'd been such a fool. All this time she'd allowed fear to dictate her life. All these years, without her even realizing it, her father had been controlling her every action, manipulating her choices from afar. Because she'd been afraid to trust herself and those around her, she'd walked when she could have run, drifted when she could have soared, hidden from the sun instead of bathing in its light—easy to do in Seattle, she was forced to admit. She'd also risked losing the most important thing in her life.

Harry.

"I'm an idiot."

Daniel simply smiled. "Yes, my dear."

"I have to get to him."

She didn't waste another second. Yanking open her personal file cabinet, she flipped to the far back and removed a folder. She tucked it under her arm, and then gathered up her purse and the envelope her uncle had given her. "Thank you, Uncle Daniel," she said, planting a kiss on his cheek. "You've been more help than you'll ever know."

He positively glowed at the praise. "It's what I do best."

"Yes, it is. And don't let anyone tell you different. Not the cops, not the judge, not even me." She practically ran from the office. Skidding to a halt beside Rosy's desk she shook the pages of her journal at her cousin. "You are so dead!"

Rosy yawned. "Yeah, yeah. Tell someone who cares. You know you're gonna thank me in the end."

"But first I'm going to kill you."

"Jones won't let you. He owes me, remember? If I hadn't sent that blueprint of yours, he'd have never come chasing after you. Now that I think about it, that means you both owe me. And don't think I won't collect." She continued before Madison had a chance to argue. "Oh, and one piece of advice before you go. Make him get down on his knees when he proposes. That's where Kent's goin' when he's done falling in love with me. Straight to his knees."

"You've got it backward." Madison spun on her heel. "I'm the one who has some groveling to do."

"That's a bad way to start a marriage and I'm puttin' that in the sequel I'm gonna write for Jones," Rosy retorted. "Chapter One... *Women don't have knees so don't expect clean floors, scrubbed toilets or any groveling.* You can tell Harry I said that, too."

Madison paused in the doorway of the parlor where her grandmother and all the Sunflowers sat. To a one, they eyed her with nervous apprehension. "Does everyone know Harry wrote his book except me?"

Sunny settled her party hat at a more rakish angle. "You mean Harry didn't tell you? I was sure he'd have done it by now. I'll have Bartholomew speak to the boy. We can't have anything but absolute honesty in your marriage. Principle number seven, in case you're interested." Leaving the couch, she crossed to Madison's side and slapped *The Principles of Love* into her hand. "Try reading it this time. Maybe if you'd done it the first time I asked, you wouldn't be having all these problems."

"Sunny?"

"Yes, love?"

"I'm lucky to have you for my grandmother." Her gaze shifted to the rest of her relatives. "I'm lucky to have all of you. Thank you for taking me in."

Sunny twinkled up at Madison. "Oh, piffle. We're the lucky ones. Where would we be without you?"

"Lost," Aunt Dell chirped up. "Totally lost."

Madison smiled through her tears. "You have that reversed, Aunt Dell. I was the one who was lost."

"Yes, yes. And now you're found." Sunny pushed her toward the front door. "We'll all have time for a big, mushy group hug after you apologize to Harry and explain why you've been such an idiot. We'll put your birthday party on hold. Bring him back for cake and ice cream after everything's settled."

Rosy snorted. "Yeah. Like there's gonna be any left. Of course if there is…" Her eyes widened. "*Ice cream!* What a great idea. I've got a new instruction for Harry."

Madison yanked open the front door. "Too late. He thought of that one ages ago."

Harry answered the door on her second knock. He was dressed in prime intimidation mode—suit, tie, lion-colored hair slicked into order. "What can I do for you, Madison?"

"Why didn't you tell me?" she demanded, brushing past him.

He stepped aside. "Please. Come in."

She retreated to the living room before turning on him. "Why didn't you tell me that my blueprint was almost identical to your principles?"

He folded his arms across his chest, his expression more remote than she'd ever seen before. "Why didn't you read my book? Then I wouldn't have had to tell you."

Darn. "Okay, you've got me there," she admitted.

"How did you find out that your blueprint and my principles matched?"

"I read your book. I've been sitting outside your hotel crying my way through it for the past two hours."

"It wasn't meant to make you cry."

"Well, it did. Though now that I think about it, I have to admit that I messed up on principle number ten. It wasn't anywhere on my blueprint." The bluster went right out of her and she looked at him with total frankness, holding nothing back. "Maybe if I'd thought of it, instead of having to live through it, I wouldn't have wasted so much time or caused such heartache. I'm sorry for that, Harry. I should have read your book sooner. It would have saved us a lot of trouble. Of course it would have caused all sorts of other problems."

His eyebrows shot up at that. "What problems?"

She shrugged. "Considering I thought your father had written *Principles,* I'd have probably dumped you and fought my grandmother for him."

For a moment she thought she'd gone too far. Then he growled a word that brought the color flooding into her cheeks and snatched her into his arms. "You drive me insane."

"I'm sorry," she whispered into his tie. "I'm so, so sorry."

"You damned well should be."

She shoved at his shoulders. Not that it did any good. "Don't get too happy," she warned when he refused to release her. "There's something I haven't told you. Something you should know about me."

"Your blueprint told me everything I needed to know."

"You're wrong." She released her breath in a long sigh, struggling to find the right words to tell him about her past. Not that there were any right words, just the truth. "You said last night that you thought we were alike, but we're not. There's one major difference between us."

"And what's that?"

"I'm not ethical like you. I'm every bit as bad as my cousin Linc. Worse, I suppose."

He stilled, a tension gathering in the arms that held her and the chest that supported her. "Explain."

She offered the folder she'd removed from her filing cabinet. "Here. This is for you." He made no move to take it from her and she tossed it onto the coffee table.

"What is it?" he asked.

"A dossier on me." The urge to run was so strong she literally shook with it. She forced herself to meet his gaze and put her faith in the man she loved with all her heart. "Do you remember my saying my father was a thief and a liar?"

"Yes."

She fought through the anguish of her confession, clinging to a desperate pride in the face of a shame she'd taken as her own. "What I failed to mention is that he also taught me how to do it."

"Taught you?" Harry captured her chin in his palm and tilted her face upward. Sunlight streamed in the picture windows, casting an ambient glow over her and baring every thought and emotion. "What do you mean, he taught you?"

She swallowed painfully. "Once he realized I possessed a nature more similar to his than to my mother's side of the family, he made sure that I became an Adams in every corrupted sense of the word."

"I don't understand."

Frustration ripped through her, a frustration that traced its roots to fear. "Don't you get it? He taught me how to embezzle money. When I was old enough to hold a job, he helped me find part-time work in businesses where I could assist him steal. I was the inside man. My job was to gather crucial information on how to get around their systems. After all, who'd suspect a kid?''

Harry said a word that she'd never heard spoken aloud. ''How old were you?''

''Sixteen.''

''But you walked away from all that.''

''Not until after they caught me.''

''Damn him!'' Harry's anger finally erupted and it was a terrifying sight. She'd never understood how much control he'd exerted until that moment. To see his wrath unleashed was to witness a storm more elemental and primitive than anything that had gone before. The word ''intimidation'' took on a whole new meaning. ''I swear, if it's the last thing I do, I'll take that man down.''

Madison clung to him, refusing to let go. To her amazement her touch acted like a balm, draining the fury from him, though she doubted it would change her father's ultimate fate. ''He's to blame for a lot of what happened to me, but not all. I was every bit as ruthless as my father. I enjoyed what he'd taught me to do. I got off on the power, the risk.''

''What convinced you to walk away? Getting caught?''

She shook her head. ''I received a slap on the wrist, courtesy of Uncle Tyler. We laughed about it afterward.''

''Then why did you leave your father?''

''Sunny called the day before my eighteenth birthday. And I suddenly realized that I'd given up on clicking my heels together and trying to get back home. I wasn't Dorothy anymore. At some point I'd turned into the Wicked Witch and I was ashamed of what I'd become. I didn't want Sunny to find out the truth. It would have devastated her. That's when something changed inside of me. That's when I decided I had to get away before every last scrap of Sunflower was plucked out of me." Time to finish it. Time to see if they still had a future. "There's more, Harry. And it's worse."

"Aw, hell." He cupped her closer, holding her as though she might shatter if he let go. "Finish it. Finish it, so we can put this behind us."

Her throat tightened to the point that she wasn't certain she could get the words out. "I'm the one who taught Linc. What happened at Bradford's isn't his fault. It's mine. He was my younger cousin and I should have protected him. Instead I—" Her voice broke, but she didn't relent. "I did my level best to corrupt him. Apparently, I succeeded."

"You're wrong, Madison. You saved him."

"What are you talking about?"

"After you left, Linc confessed to everything. He also gave us information that should put an end to your father's career. And he asked us to help him. He said you'd managed to get away from the Adams and would we be willing to help him get away, too." Harry forked his hands into her hair, her curls clinging to his fingers in joyous abandon. "He didn't betray you, Madison. He never said a word about your past. And when he talked about you, it was with admiration. You're an example to him, sweetheart. An example that may make all the difference to his future."

She was crying by the time he'd finished. "I've been so afraid. Afraid to trust people in case they found out I wasn't what I seemed. Afraid to believe in permanence in case it was taken away from me, like when my parents divorced. Afraid to lose control of the people I love in case they leave."

"You're talking about Sunny."

She nodded, the tears coming faster. "I panicked when I found out about your father. They were going to marry and move east together. And...and I couldn't stand the thought of losing her. The Sunflower family is my safety net. My protection. If something happened to them, I was terrified that I might turn into an Adams again."

"That will never happen."

"I know that now." She clutched the lapels of his suit jacket. "Harry?"

A tender light appeared in his eyes and it gave her hope. "What is it, honey?"

"I love you."

"It took you a long time to figure that out, didn't it?"

"Far too long. Is it too late? For us, I mean?"

"How can you even ask me that?" His mouth closed over hers in a kiss of such passion she prayed it would never end. "I love you, Madison. I fell in love with you after reading the first few words you wrote in your journal. And I fell even harder when we sat on a stuck elevator and I held you in my arms."

"Despite the fact that I'd trashed your book?"

"Maybe because of it. I knew that if you hadn't read it, you couldn't have been influenced by it. What you'd put in your journal had to have come from your heart and soul. I also knew that I wanted the woman who'd written those words because they echoed my own thoughts and dreams."

"I have another confession to make," she admitted.

"And what's that?"

"I think I fell in love with you that first day on the elevator."

It was so good to see the humor return to his eyes. "Love at first hearing?"

"At first hearing, at first touch. But most of all at first kindness and first kiss." She wrapped her arms around his neck. "I believe in you, Harry. I believe in your book and in your integrity and your love."

He released a bone-deep sigh of sheer contentment. "Does that mean you're not afraid to make a commitment, anymore?"

"Commitment?" She grinned. "Piffle. No problem at all. To quote a very intimidating man, 'I want to start at once-upon-a-time with you and go straight through until we reach happily-ever-after.'"

"In that case..." He lifted her into his arms. "We'd better get started right away. Because I have a lot of once-upon-a-time to work through with you."

She snuggled close. "Then I suggest a brief detour to the dining room. I have more leaves to pluck."

"Palm fronds, my love. Palm fronds."

NEARLYWEDS

Almost at the altar— will these *nearlyweds* become *newlyweds*?

Harlequin Romance® is delighted to invite you to some special weddings! Yet these are no ordinary weddings. Our beautiful brides and gorgeous grooms only *nearly* make it to the altar—before fate intervenes.

But the story doesn't end there....
Find out what happens in these tantalizingly emotional novels!

Authors to look out for include:

Leigh Michaels—The Bridal Swap
Liz Fielding—His Runaway Bride
Janelle Denison—The Wedding Secret
Renee Roszel—Finally a Groom
Caroline Anderson—The Impetuous Bride

Available wherever Harlequin books are sold.

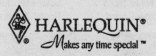

HARLEQUIN®
Makes any time special ™

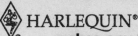

Harlequin truly does make any time special.... This year we are celebrating weddings in style!

To help us celebrate, we want you to tell us how wearing the Harlequin wedding gown will make your wedding day special. As the grand prize, Harlequin will offer one lucky bride the chance to **"Walk Down the Aisle" in the Harlequin wedding gown!**

There's more...

For her honeymoon, she and her groom will spend five nights at the **Hyatt Regency Maui.** As part of this five-night honeymoon at the hotel renowned for its romantic attractions, the couple will enjoy a candlelit dinner for two in Swan Court, a sunset sail on the hotel's catamaran, and duet spa treatments.

Maui • Molokai • Lanai

To enter, please write, in, 250 words or less, how wearing the Harlequin wedding gown will make your wedding day special. The entry will be judged based on its emotionally compelling nature, its originality and creativity, and its sincerity. This contest is open to Canadian and U.S. residents only and to those who are 18 years of age and older. There is no purchase necessary to enter. Void where prohibited. See further contest rules attached. Please send your entry to:

Walk Down the Aisle Contest

In Canada	In U.S.A.
P.O. Box 637	P.O. Box 9076
Fort Erie, Ontario	3010 Walden Ave.
L2A 5X3	Buffalo, NY 14269-9076

You can also enter by visiting www.eHarlequin.com
Win the Harlequin wedding gown and the vacation of a lifetime!
The deadline for entries is October 1, 2001.

Makes any time special ®

PHWDACONT1

HARLEQUIN WALK DOWN THE AISLE TO MAUI CONTEST 1197
OFFICIAL RULES
NO PURCHASE NECESSARY TO ENTER

1. To enter, follow directions published in the offer to which you are responding. Contest begins April 2, 2001, and ends on October 1, 2001. Method of entry may vary. Mailed entries must be postmarked by October 1, 2001, and received by October 8, 2001.

2. Contest entry may be, at times, presented via the Internet, but will be restricted solely to residents of certain geographic areas that are disclosed on the Web site. To enter via the Internet, if permissible, access the Harlequin Web site (www.eHarlequin.com) and follow the directions displayed online. Online entries must be received by 11:59 p.m. E.S.T. on October 1, 2001.

   In lieu of submitting an entry online, enter by mail by hand-printing (or typing) on an 8½" x 11" plain piece of paper, your name, address (including zip code), Contest number/name and in 250 words or fewer, why winning a Harlequin wedding dress would make your wedding day special. Mail via first-class mail to: Harlequin Walk Down the Aisle Contest 1197, (in the U.S.) P.O. Box 9076, 3010 Walden Avenue, Buffalo, NY 14269-9076, (in Canada) P.O. Box 637, Fort Erie, Ontario L2A 5X3, Canada.

   Limit one entry per person, household address and e-mail address. Online and/or mailed entries received from persons residing in geographic areas in which Internet entry is not permissible will be disqualified.

3. Contests will be judged by a panel of members of the Harlequin editorial, marketing and public relations staff based on the following criteria:

   • Originality and Creativity—50%
   • Emotionally Compelling—25%
   • Sincerity—25%

   In the event of a tie, duplicate prizes will be awarded. Decisions of the judges are final.

4. All entries become the property of Torstar Corp. and will not be returned. No responsibility is assumed for lost, late, illegible, incomplete, inaccurate, nondelivered or misdirected mail or misdirected e-mail, for technical, hardware or software failures of any kind, lost or unavailable network connections, or failed, incomplete, garbled or delayed computer transmission or any human error which may occur in the receipt or processing of the entries in this Contest.

5. Contest open only to residents of the U.S. (except Puerto Rico) and Canada, who are 18 years of age or older, and is void wherever prohibited by law; all applicable laws and regulations apply. Any litigation within the Province of Quebec respecting the conduct or organization of a publicity contest may be submitted to the Régie des alcools, des courses et des jeux for a ruling. Any litigation respecting the awarding of a prize may be submitted to the Régie des alcools, des courses et des jeux or for the purpose of helping the parties reach a settlement. Employees and immediate family members of Torstar Corp. and D. L. Blair, Inc., their affiliates, subsidiaries and all other agencies, entities and persons connected with the use, marketing or conduct of this Contest are not eligible to enter. Taxes on prizes are the sole responsibility of winners. Acceptance of any prize offered constitutes permission to use winner's name, photograph or other likeness for the purposes of advertising, trade and promotion on behalf of Torstar Corp., its affiliates and subsidiaries without further compensation to the winner, unless prohibited by law.

6. Winners will be determined no later than November 15, 2001, and will be notified by mail. Winners will be required to sign and return an Affidavit of Eligibility form within 15 days after winner notification. Noncompliance within that time period may result in disqualification and an alternative winner may be selected. Winners of trip must execute a Release of Liability prior to ticketing and must possess required travel documents (e.g. passport, photo ID) where applicable. Trip must be completed by November 2002. No substitution of prize permitted by winner. Torstar Corp. and D. L. Blair, Inc., their parents, affiliates, and subsidiaries are not responsible for errors in printing or electronic presentation of Contest, entries and/or game pieces. In the event of printing or other errors which may result in unintended prize values or duplication of prizes, all affected game pieces or entries shall be null and void. If for any reason the Internet portion of the Contest is not capable of running as planned, including infection by computer virus, bugs, tampering, unauthorized intervention, fraud, technical failures, or any other causes beyond the control of Torstar Corp. which corrupt or affect the administration, secrecy, fairness, integrity or proper conduct of the Contest, Torstar Corp. reserves the right, at its sole discretion, to disqualify any individual who tampers with the entry process and to cancel, terminate, modify or suspend the Contest or the Internet portion thereof. In the event of a dispute regarding an online entry, the entry will be deemed submitted by the authorized holder of the e-mail account submitted at the time of entry. Authorized account holder is defined as the natural person who is assigned to an e-mail address by an Internet access provider, online service provider or other organization that is responsible for arranging e-mail address for the domain associated with the submitted e-mail address. **Purchase or acceptance of a product offer does not improve your chances of winning.**

7. Prizes: (1) Grand Prize—A Harlequin wedding dress (approximate retail value: $3,500) and a 5-night/6-day honeymoon trip to Maui, HI, including round-trip air transportation provided by Maui Visitors Bureau from Los Angeles International Airport (winner is responsible for transportation to and from Los Angeles International Airport) and a Harlequin Romance Package, including hotel accomodations (double occupancy) at the Hyatt Regency Maui Resort and Spa, dinner for (2) two at Swan Court, a sunset sail on Kiele V and a spa treatment for the winner (approximate retail value: $4,000); (5) Five runner-up prizes of a $1000 gift certificate to selected retail outlets to be determined by Sponsor (retail value $1000 ea.). Prizes consist of only those items listed as part of the prize. Limit one prize per person. All prizes are valued in U.S. currency.

8. For a list of winners (available after December 17, 2001) send a self-addressed, stamped envelope to: Harlequin Walk Down the Aisle Contest 1197 Winners, P.O. Box 4200 Blair, NE 68009-4200 or you may access the www.eHarlequin.com Web site through January 15, 2002.

Contest sponsored by Torstar Corp., P.O. Box 9042, Buffalo, NY 14269-9042, U.S.A.

PHWDACONT2

**What happens when you suddenly
discover your happy twosome is about
to turn into a...*family*?
Do you laugh?
Do you cry?
Or...do you get married?**

The answer is all of the above—and plenty more!

Share the laughter and tears with
Harlequin Romance® as these
unsuspecting couples have to be

When parenthood takes you by surprise!

Authors to look out for include:

**Caroline Anderson—DELIVERED: ONE FAMILY
Barbara McMahon—TEMPORARY FATHER
Grace Green—TWINS INCLUDED!
Liz Fielding—THE BACHELOR'S BABY**

Available wherever Harlequin books are sold.

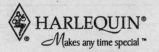

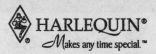

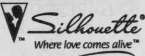